BY MAURICE CARLOS RUFFIN

The Ones Who Don't Say They Love You

We Cast a Shadow

THE ONES WHO DON'T SAY THEY LOVE YOU

THE ONES
WHO DON'T
SAY THEY
LOVE YOU

STORIES

MAURICE
CARLOS
RUFFIN

ONE WORLD
NEW YORK

Copyright © 2021 by Maurice Carlos Ruffin

Published in the United States by One World, an imprint of
Random House, a division of Penguin Random House LLC, New York.

ONE WORLD and colophon are registered trademarks of
Penguin Random House LLC.

Some of the stories in this work were originally published in
*Apalachee Review, The Iowa Review, Kenyon Review, The Pinch,
Redivider Journal, Slant,* and *South Carolina Review.*

Library of Congress Cataloging-in-Publication Data
Names: Ruffin, Maurice Carlos, author.
Title: The ones who don't say they love you : stories /
Maurice Carlos Ruffin. Other titles:
The ones who do not say they love you
Description: First edition. | New York : One World, 2021
Identifiers: LCCN 2020048605 (print) |
LCCN 2020048606 (ebook) |
ISBN 9780593133408 (hardcover; acid-free paper) |
ISBN 9780593133422 (ebook)
Subjects: LCSH: New Orleans (La.)—Fiction. | LCGFT: Short stories.
Classification: LCC PS3618.U4338 R84 2021 (print) | LCC PS3618.
U4338 (ebook) | DDC 813/.6—dc23
LC record available at https://lccn.loc.gov/2020048605

Printed in Canada on acid-free paper

oneworldlit.com
randomhousebooks.com

1 2 3 4 5 6 7 8 9

First Edition

Book design by Susan Turner

For Tanzanika and the children of New Orleans

In New Orleans, culture doesn't come down from on high,
it bubbles up from the street.

—Ellis Marsalis

Contents

THE ONES WHO DON'T SAY THEY LOVE YOU

The Ones Who Don't Say They Love You

You on the sidewalk out front of the convenience store. The sun beat down like it do every morning. The street cleaner pass by spraying lemonade-smelling water. It get on your tennis shoes, shoes that's coming loose at the heel, so your socks get wet, too. Soapy water drip down the curb. Not like this street stay clean long.

Mr. Jellnik round the corner like he being dogged. He ain't much to look at. They never is. He like the other men who come down for foot-fixing conventions and brain-fixing conventions. He got a fat neck and skin like old peaches. His wallet fat, too; that all you care about.

Jellnik eye you from crotch to mouth. He pull out a pack. He smoke. You pull one from the pack and light yours with his.

"Why are you the only one out here this morning?" He cover his eyes halfway. The sun glare off the Mississippi River Bridge like *I see you, boy.*

"I'm the onliest one you need," you say.

"True enough."

The other tappers already off to work, probably almost done with the men they left with. They left you with the tip box. The box is for your protection. You wear bottle caps on your soles and dance so people think you and the others are cymbal monkeys.

A police car roll up the street. The lights flash blue white blue, but the car don't slow down even though the cop lean over to get a eyeful of your faces. Jellnik's butt cheeks tense up. You could tell him don't sweat it, but you like seeing him squirm. If you didn't like seeing him squirm, you would tell him cops never arrest johns, especially not johns from Ida-fucking-ho. What you do probably make the cops puke, make them stay away. It's easy to lock up dudes for shooting dudes. That's good business. Putting a junior high slut in jail is bad business. If they hear all about what you do, people stop coming to town. You all starve then.

The stoplight turn green. The police car pull off. Jellnik's ass relax. You don't really need to tap-dance to stay out of jail. But if you don't at least fake it, what else you got?

Jellnik the only one who buy you food after he do his business. Now, you sore inside and out, but you starving, too. The queenie cook behind the counter flipping pancakes.

Maybe the pancakes'll take your mind off how rough Jellnik handle you.

Jellnik's toast and runny eggs come out first. He squirt ketchup all over. He gulp coffee, get a refill, gulp that, too. He don't give you none. Your stomach growl. When you bring food to the corner, the other tappers take most of it, leave you the scrap. Most days you don't eat till you go home. But today you hungry. What the shit is the holdup? The queenie cook went in back and your pancake sitting on the cold side of the grill like a Frisbee that just stop spinning.

Jellnik been here all week. The first day he show up, he take Pink and Quincy first, one in the morning and the other round lunch. He come back for you after noontime, rocking up the street with hair stuck to his forehead. After he take a piece of you, he never buy what Pink and Quincy selling again. That's a plus on top of the money. It's the only time you won out when they around. You too dark and your hair ain't good and wavy like Pink hair. But now you can laugh inside when you see them. You can't laugh out loud. They punch you if you smile.

Jellnik break out a roll of cash. He put down two twenty-dollar bills. One for the food and one for you. Twenty won't cover the food, so that'll come out of what you earn.

"When I leave tonight," Jellnik say. "I want you to come with me."

He pour sugar in his coffee. His finger got ketchup on it that he don't see. He stir his coffee with that finger.

"I'll get you a plane ticket, and I have a storage unit you can stay in until we find you something more appropriate."

"Man," you say, "I ain't going to nobody Idaho."

"Listen to me," he say, "you can do better than this place. It's not safe for you."

"Nobody mess with me round here," you say.

He put a hand on your face where you bruised from when Pink hit you the other day. You like to flinch away, but you don't 'cause his hand feel warm.

"You don't know anything," Jellnik say. "I've been visiting New Orleans for over twenty years. You think you're one of the first boys to stand on that corner? What do you think happened to the boys who were there before you?"

You could tell Jellnik about Pink's brother, Simmy, who went puff like match smoke last month. Simmy was the first one you met when you came out here. He looked out for you, but now he gone. You know he ain't go to Idaho.

"Why you care about what happen to me?" you ask.

"Just be back at the corner around six P.M. with your personal belongings. I'll be in a gray sport utility vehicle."

When Jellnik get up, the stool squeal like it being stabbed. By then, your pancake black and crusty, still dying on that grill.

The queenie cook wearing mascara and hoop earrings, so you know he a full-on Mary. He flip the pancake to your plate. He smack the plate down. Sound like it crack, but it don't. He shake his head at you like he better than you. You want to jump over the counter and stomp his face on the grill. Or make him suck your junk. You want to make him say your name like he mean it. But he grown. He break you in five pieces, if you try. You be on the wrong end like always.

The pancake darker than you. You don't touch it.

You snatch all the money and run. The cook yell after you, but those just words.

. . .

When you go into the house with a box of chicken and biscuits, Lorraine back early from the casino downtown. She in her spot in front of the TV. She don't have no legs. You bought toilet paper and chocolate milk, too. You unpack the groceries. She don't look up. She eating a bag of orange puffs. Her lips orange. She keep them on her lap so the little kids won't get none. None of you like to get close to her. She grab too hard.

You go to the kitchen and put the chicken down. You yell out the back door for the little boys rolling in the grass by the flat-tire pickup truck. The boys are foster boys like you. Lorraine get a check every two weeks for keeping y'all. You don't get any because she call it rent. She take rent to the casino. If she win, she don't tell you.

"You better find your own," she always say. But she eat what you bring home. Her cut she call it.

You go back to the kitchen. You open the box and a roach in it. The little boys come in the back door, screaming and smacking each other. You can't let them see that roach because then they won't eat. You don't have money to buy more, and the little bit of chicken you brought ain't enough for them anyway. You pop the bug in your mouth.

Jellnik's storage shed must be pretty big. A big man wouldn't have a small shed. A big man would have a shed big enough to do cartwheels in. His condo in the French Quarter is small. But everything in the French Quarter small. If everything was big, it would be the French Dollar. When he put you in position, you stare out the window. There's a tree outside with heart-shaped leaves. You count those leaves. You never get past fifteen. In all the times you done business with Jellnik, he never say he love you. That's the only reason you listen to him at all. The other ones always say they love you.

You don't want to see Pink and Quincy at the corner, instead they over there tap-dancing extra fast. They trying to wring the last little bit of pocket change out of the tourists before it get dark. The cops won't take you in for hustling johns, but they don't stand for curfew breakers. It don't look right for tappers to be on the street after dark. What don't look right is bad for business. Bottle caps scraping concrete make you sick like you ate a crate full of bottle caps. You wonder where Jellnik at. It's after time. You wonder if you feel better when he come around.

"Where you been at?" Quincy say.

"Not making any, I bet," Pink say. "Ain't never got his shit together, this baby here."

You tell them to suck a horse and they howl.

"You a salty little bitch today," Pink say. "You slow?"

You tell them you ain't slow. You tell them you about to get paid. You tell them you leaving with Jellnik as soon as he get here.

"Humpty Dumpty?" Quincy frown.

"That man ain't bringing you nowheres, boy," Pink say.

A gray SUV down the block. It look like it going to turn before it make it to you. You stop looking.

Quincy pinch your shoulder. "You're serious, ain't you, baby?"

"He coming for me," you say.

"I bet you twenty he ain't," Pink say.

Pink wrestle you and snatch your last from your pocket. It's only a five. Pink say that'll do until you get more. You tell him you ain't lost yet. Pink say he good for the night and leave with your five.

You only have one bottle cap for your shoe, but you going to pass some time tapping. Make some change to buy a cold drink because your mouth taste like funk. You dance until that cap break loose and roll into the gutter.

Something flash. A police car creep your way. The lights beep slow, but the car speed up. You can't see the cop driving, but hands in cuffs press on the back seat glass. Jellnik face behind those hands.

Cocoon

My father named his bug company "Stevens and Son" even before I came into the world. I found insects disgusting, but it was just me and him, so I did my best to keep my objections hidden. I certainly never told him about my proclivities.

I was a pretty good bug man in my teens and could tell what the infestation was by the faintest clues. Teeny tiny scratch marks on a pantry shelf were the sign of a mouse, for example. Whenever we came across something we'd never seen before—like that bellows-shaped mud nest in Ms. Berthelot's attic—I was the first to guess and was nearly always right. They were mud wasps. The males sipped nectar on swamp azaleas while the females built houses with their mouths.

Still, I grew tired of spending my weekends hunting vermin. My father was in his sixties and needed someone who would really put his back into the work. That's why he hired Tyronne Myers. Tyronne was into it. I had the impression that he had lived a hard life somewhere else. Yet, whenever I asked him about his past he just placed a hand on my shoulder, a situation I very much enjoyed, and chuckled.

"Can't stay wrapped in what you come from," he'd say.

I was in my bedroom one night, alone I thought, when I sensed Tyronne near the door. I don't know if he saw me, in front of my mirror in a calico dress I'd bought at the thrift store on Carrollton Avenue. Quickly, I switched off the lamp, slipped on jeans in the dark, and left the house to meet my friends. The next morning, I quit. My father showed no emotion, but he took sick a year later and sold the company to Tyronne.

Years after I moved to New York to pursue a career in fashion design, I went back home. Tyronne never changed the name of the company and, to my surprise, he didn't seem shocked to see me with hair extensions and wearing a crinkled suede waistcoat of my creation. He invited me into the house he was servicing to show me something he had found. He stooped and gave me a ghostly thing, lighter than a feather and so thin the lines on the palm of my hand were clearly visible through it.

"Do you know what that is?" he asked.

"It's what moths come from," I said.

Beg Borrow Steal

The first thing Pop do when he get home from Angola is shove you and your little sister out the front door. He don't even say hi. He just tell Mama to please give him a dollar for you to get huckabucks. Mama tell him he got nerve telling her what to do with her dollar when she been trying to pay the bills all by herself for twenty-three and a half months and five days. The lights been out since last night, so how 'bout earning a dollar? That one vein in the crook of Pop elbow pulse like a fat worm. He say you know I love you, baby. He push past Mama, borrow a five from her purse, and tell you not to come back till the streetlights light up. You and Timithea head over to the Johnsons', who sell chips, cold drinks, and everything out they house on weekends, but the back window down and the curtains drawn, too, so they ain't open. Before long you and Timithea end up where the community center was before it burned. Full dump trucks wait like big, dumb elephants. You never do get those huckabucks.

You and Timithea go back to the house but sit on the back porch floor and watch boxcars clank together. Timithea's hair barrette done fell loose, and she look agitated. You don't know how to fix it, so you throw down your bouncy ball and let her chase it. She a lot more fun now that she more than a honeydew melon wrapped in swaddling. Even more fun than that mutt dog you had for a day that one time.

Pop open the back door, run his hand over your head, and say we going. You ask where.

Mama's standing behind him smiling, and that make you smile.

Just do what you told, she say. But she don't say it mean. Pop grab the necklace, a wire-thin gold chain with a teardrop pearl, round Mama's neck. His fingers pulling at it, so it's taut, but doesn't break from around her neck.

Where the rest of that good jewelry I got you?

I sold it, Mama say.

All of it? he ask.

It's what I had to do, Mama say.

Pop nod. I see that, he say.

Mama pick up Timithea and do that thing with her hand to check Timithea's diaper like checking a pear to see if it ready to eat.

Pop whistle as we walk from the backyard to the front of the house. He toss the keys at you.

You want to drive? he ask.

Serious? you ask.

It's Mama car that she bought with her money. The thing got a spoiler on the back hatch and pink dice hanging like cherries from the mirror. She don't even like Pop driving it. But maybe everything different now.

Fight me for it, he say. We wrestle on our feet, laughing the whole time. He put you in a headlock, but you hold that key tight in your fist. When you get behind the wheel, he shaking his head and frowning.

Get out, he say.

Why?

I thought you'd be taller by now. Instead, you just got fat. Your feet barely come down to the floorboard.

You don't move, but just keep your hands on the wheel. A bug crash into the front glass.

It flutter for a sec like it's trying to figure what the shit just happen. Then it spins away.

Just around the block, you say. Pop smack the back of your head hard enough to make you fuzzy.

I don't have time for game playing. You think I'm about to go back to that cage on account of letting a ten-year-old drive?

Pop drive you to a couple of places round town. First, to the supermarket where lobsters chop at the glass tank like they saying help man get me out of this place. The manager there know Pop and say he can't take on no felon. That ain't him. That's policy from on high. Then Pop drive to the used-tire garage, but the men there don't even let him out the car. They bang on the hood and tell Pop to get ghost

15

before they bust him in the mouth. One of the men come over to Pop open window. He got one gold tooth, but the tooth next to it missing.

I'd cap you right now if your offspring wasn't with you, the man say. He kick the car door, and Pop shout, but we drive away.

You go to Robinson Pizza under the highway bridge. Inside, Mr. Robinson come out from behind the counter. Something crawl by, and Mr. Robinson step on it. He see Pop and throw his hands up.

I don't want no trouble, Timmy, Mr. Robinson say. Pop frown at Mr. Robinson. Then Mr. Robinson tap him on the jaw real light. They hug. Pop say something in Mr. Robinson ear. Mr. Robinson slap Pop back and tell you hey, little Tim, you gonna be a sumo wrestler one day.

I need to make some money, Pop say. Lights due. Rent due. Life due.

Kitchen Sink Tyrone got sent to federal lockup in Mississippi, Mr. Robinson say. And nobody ain't seen Jupe since Christmas. Jupe was Pop best friend. The last time you saw him he and Pop showed you how to crack open a steering wheel column and hot-wire a car.

No, Pop say, not that kind of money. Mr. Robinson raise his eyebrow. You for real?

Can't a man change his hustle? I want to pay taxes and shit. Is that wrong? If I could sell my blood, I would, but I ain't got that much blood. You feel me? Mr. Robinson pinch Pop shoulder and wink at you.

Your old man growing up, son.

* * *

Pop can cook, but Mr. Robinson's kitchen full up. That's why you and Pop riding up the avenue to where all the white college dorms at. You got hot pizza and breadsticks on your lap. It smell good and you want to grab a bite of something, so you reach in and pinch a hunk of pineapple and anchovies. Who the shit order pineapple and anchovies? You don't want Pop to see what you did so you eat the nasty stuff. It burn the roof of your mouth.

Pop stuck a Robinson Pizza sign on the roof of Mama car. The sign keep slapping the roof. Wuk. Wuk. Wuk. The back of your head still hurt. Now your mouth hurt, too, and your stomach gurgling from the fruit and fish fighting inside.

Pop park by a big house with symbols on the front you can't read. Make you feel stupid, and you don't like that feeling, so you make up a meaning for them. Crazy White People.

You follow Pop up the stairs to the house, holding the pizza box. A boy with a belt wrapped round his head answer the door. He call back for somebody named Charlie, and a white girl come to the door. Her eyes open, but she looking woozy like she dreaming on her feet.

Hold it, Mr. Cosby, she say real slow. I have to give you a proper pourboire.

Somebody in the house yell out *What, no Jell-O pudding pops?* The girl flip through some money and count off dollars one by one, all the way to seventeen. She shut the door. Pop grin.

You ain't use to Pop grinning so much at least not without the feeling something bad about to happen. When you asked Mama if y'all could see Pop in prison she said no. She said prison was just a way for rich people to decide who was the worst people and by deciding that, and locking them up, they could stay rich and on top. And that seeing Pop would mess up your head too much. They treated men like dogs, running them from food bowl to water bowl to the yard where they barked at each other. You wonder if when someone free of that kind of living it make somebody smile more.

That's an alright tip, Pop say. Pop turn quick from the steps of the house toward the car and yell. *Hey! What you doing by my car?*

A white boy in a baseball cap is sitting in the driver seat. He crank the engine, and the back tire spin before the car move. Pop a fast runner, but he only get a little way down the street before Mama car out of reach.

At the police station, Pop talk to a cop for a while. You don't like being in the station, but Pop say it's about time the cops do something to help him for a change. A skinny cop at the desk tell him they'll look into it, but not to get his hopes up. A man in a black suit comes around the corner and seeing Pop calls his name. The man look like a funeral man. Pop don't look him in the eye.

I didn't expect to see you back here so soon, Funeral Man say. You people just can't fly right, can you?

Pop tell him about the car. Funeral Man snort.

Well, was it retaliation? Funeral Man say. What goes around. He makes a circle with his finger.

I ain't got to take this, Pop say, and pull you up from the chair you sitting on by your elbow.

You'll take what I give you, Funeral Man say. Causing trouble is a violation of your parole. I can have you back in central lockup before your kid bellies up for fried chicken tonight.

Outside, Pop walk away from the station real quick. You get out of breath trying to keep up, and you can't. His legs too long. Your legs too short. He stop around the corner and shove the meaty part of his hands in his eyes.

You shoulda punched him, you say.

You think I deserved to go away like I did? To prison?

No, Pop. They did you wrong 'cause they could.

I did me wrong, he say. Don't be a dummy. You know I stole stuff. They didn't even get me for half what I took.

But you just borrowed that, you say. Pop told you a long time ago the difference between borrowing and stealing. Thieves steal 'cause they heartless and like to hurt people. Good people like him borrow because they need it more than who they taking from. Good people give to others. Like how Pop gave all that jewelry to Mama.

I took a ring, Pop say. A real pretty ring with emeralds set in the side for your Mama, but lost it running away that night they got me. I did what I did and took my lick. But I need you to listen to me. You listening? Just because I messed up don't mean I can't be somebody else now.

It's a long walk from the police station to the horse race-track, but you get there fast. Chop Shop Alley, Pop call it. A bunch of garages lined up shoulder to shoulder. This was Pop and Jupe hangout spot. Two dudes talk by the garage farthest down. One of them is the white boy with the base-ball cap. Pop start running, you follow, but trip on the gravel. The baseball hat white boy see Pop and run to the back, where Mama car is. Pop can't see where he went, but he hear the car start up and the crunch of the gravel as it speeds off. Mama car gone again.

Pop goes after the other dude, holding him by the arm. Pop ask the dude where Baseball Cap live.

Who? the guy say and shrug Pop hand off his arm.

Why you playing stupid? Pop ask. The cat you was just talking to.

I don't know him. He asked if I had a lighter, but I don't smoke.

Your feet tired from all the walking.

Maybe he already gave it to another chop shop, you say. Maybe we just too late. Maybe we should just go tell Mama. She might—

Pop pop you in the back of the head again. It makes you stumble, but you make sure you don't stop walking.

And you better not cry, Pop say. And even though your eyes want to let go, you don't cry.

After a while, Pop put an arm around your shoulder. He rub the side of your head.

I don't mean to do that so hard, he say. Let's go in there, he say in front of Cherry's Restaurant. You go in and Pop order ribs and Cokes, and you tear those ribs up quick, eat some greens, and wash it all down. The table next to you full of people, like a family reunion or something. They waitress bring out a big cart of desserts with dishes of bread pudding and pecan pie. You know some of that would set the pounding in your head straight, but you know better than to ask for dessert.

You almost home, when you and Pop walk past a block party happening. Cars are parked all around. Fancy cars with fancy rims. Hoopties with garbage bags over the back windows. Pickups. Station wagons. It's like every car in the world here.

A few blocks away in front of a liquor store, there's a car kind of like Mama's. Only it's newer, and the tires shiny like they was just washed. Pop go to the car and graze the window with his hand like he stroking a kitten.

When we get home and tell Mama what happen, she ask what kind of man get home from prison for not even a whole day and manage to make things worse. She say she can't live like this. Pop sit at the kitchen table, next to a candle, with his hand over his eyes.

Timithea crying 'cause she hate the dark. You hate the dark, too, but you hate how hot it is with no AC even more. A light glow into your room from outside. The family next door TV on, and light and laughing come through your window from they window. You get up. You get the rod and screwdriver you keep under your bed and climb out the window. On the way down, your shirt tear on the hurricane fence, and you know Mama gonna kill you for ruining good clothes, but you also know you about to make it up.

You walk back to where that look-alike car was, and it's still there. You slide the rod into the gap between the window and the door. You feel the rod catch like you found the lock, but the door don't come open. You push the rod deeper. Nothing move. You check, but nobody watching you. A car with a broken window worth almost as much as a normal one. You find a brick on the street. The brick heavy enough to break the window without even throwing it hard.

But first you try the door, you pull it, and it open. You get in the car and shut the door. You jam the screwdriver into the steering wheel column quick and you feel something give.

Mercury Forges

My job was to make sure Mercury Forges didn't escape. He was a stocky black guy in for drugs and guns. He'd gotten out of the Orleans Parish Prison twice and no one knew how he did it.

Funny thing is he got captured within a few blocks of the prison both times.

"I get turned around when I get out there, Deputy Benoit," Mercury said once, "but I'll get free for good, just you wait."

When the hurricane hit and flooded everything, we brought the inmates out to the Broad Street overpass. I wasn't too panicked because one of the other deputies, Ronnie Dismas, said our families had made it out of town before the water came. It'd be easy to look after myself with them out of harm's way.

Mercury snuck away as soon as I turned my back. He was in a pirogue about five blocks away, bobbing like an apple. I ran across the overpass and climbed down some scaffolding to his boat, which I grabbed. We hadn't cuffed any of the inmates. It would have been impossible to move them with all the climbing we had to do to get to dry land.

"Where do you think you're going?" I asked. I had a hand on my sidearm.

"Got to find Humanity Street," he said. "That's where my pops lives." I knew his dad. A good guy who delivered the food plates we deputies ate for lunch. I liked his dad. But that shouldn't have mattered at the moment.

I can't really tell you why I didn't make him bring us back to the detention area. After a while, we floated up to a yellow house with floodwater almost to the awning.

Mercury yanked a metal pole from the water, broke through the attic window, and climbed in. There was shuffling inside and I wondered if I should go in after him. I thought this might be part of his big getaway plan, but soon he grunted out of the window and pulled his father's body out wrapped in a heavy blanket. The old man hadn't had a chance.

"Bring us back, Dep," said Mercury. And that was what I did.

Caesara Pittman, or a Negress of God

Do you, Miss Caesara Pittman, in the year of our Lord eighteen hundred and sixty-six, aver to tell the truth, the whole truth, and nothing but the truth?" Davidson, the attorney of the City of New Orleans, asks. It's hot outside and hot in the courtroom. Too hot for so many people to be on those benches, close as piglets on a mama pig's teats.

I touch the Good Book, my fingers touching on the gold edges. That man, Buford—now I know his family name—sits at the table by his own lawyer, who wears those round glasses. Buford's eyes wide with hate. He making all kind of faces at me. With those stitches down his cheek, looks like he's Lucifer hisself. But this book never sent me wrong. I place my hand on my left breast.

"Yessuh, I do," I say. "I promise on my very heart."

"Where were you on the evening of Wednesday, July 25, 1866?" Davidson rests his hands behind his back, making his belly stick out some. He's more than a couple of feet away. But I smell talc and pipe tobacco every time he pass by.

"As you say, mister. It was Wednesday, and I was down on Good Children Street to buy baguettes. I make bread pudding for my husband and young ones on Saturdays."

"On Saturdays?" Davidson's curled mustache shakes.

"You got to let it stale up good before you use it."

"Of course." Davidson laughs. Some of my folk in the gallery laugh good, too.

"It was long about sunset . . ." I wasn't far from home, had a basket on my arm. Had left the butcher where I cut offal for other free Creoles like myself. Had just passed the barn where they keep the streetcar mules when footsteps made themselves known to me. Some girls had been handled wrong lately. And some of them had been shamefully desecrated.

"I didn't come down here for no Devil work," I said, hoping to be heard. A man came out the shadow. Under the gaslight, this white man wore the clothing of a man of God. A white collar around his neck. A cross hanging underneath that.

"Just taking note of one of our Father's children." In the light, he rubbed his hands like he was cold.

But he had big shoulders and big, rough grabbing hands. The kind of hands that plowed soil or worked a cargo ship. Not the kind of hands that prayed over the sick or baptized little ones. I held my hand out, palm up. "You ain't no kind of priest."

He smiled, all the yellow teeth in his mouth shining at me. Looked like a mouth full of kernels.

"I don't take offense in the ignorance of your kind none," he said. And I wondered if I was wrong about who he might be. But I thought on the book and words came to my mouth.

And I saith: "Take no part in the unfruitful works of darkness, but instead expose them."

"What?"

"I rebuke you!" I knew enough to know that a priest should have got a twinkle in his eye when you said the Scripture to him. But this heathen's eyes stayed black. He might as well have been deaf. I dropped my basket and ran. I was fast but got tangled in my skirts. Fell on those cobblestones. Hurt my wrist.

He fell on top me, clawing at my clothes. Pushed me on my back. He pulled at my chignon. That made me madder than what I already had reason to be mad about. He shouldn't have done it. But, the exacerbated madness reminded me of the poultry knife I kept in my hair. I bought my manumission five years before the war. I was a free woman, but that didn't mean I didn't have to prove it from time to time. When slave traders needled me, I had my papers in one hand and my shiny little knife in the other.

This man's sick breath was on my face, and he was yanking my skirt. So, I jugged that knife in right under his left eye and drug it down to his lip. I smelled the metal that's in blood. He yowled like a pitiful li'l dog. If I would have drug up instead of down, I could have popped his eyeball out like a—

Davidson raises his arm. "Thank you, Miss Pittman. That will do enough. We do not wish to give the jury night terrors."

I huffed.

"What about my terrors?" I say, but he don't hear.

Davidson points at Buford. "Is this the man who accosted you?" Buford still making faces. He ugly as a pot of chitlings. His outside match his insides. I like that I did that to him.

Outside the courtroom window, the paddleboat toots. I watch a colored man throw bread at a duck. Some changes done happened since the war between the states. I was a slave most of my life working the house on a plantation up near St. Francisville. I ain't a slave no more, but I know these people in the juror box. Few of them would have wished any of us found freedom. Mr. Barker with the ruddy red cheeks sells candles and other fine things. The man with the mutton chops runs carriages. The dandy one on the end is from Virginia, almost a carpetbagger. Virginians used to sell my people to New Orleans for punishment. They hoped heat and terror work would kill us all. And then there's all the marching men the white mob killed at the convention not long after my meeting with Buford. The whites trapped the good men inside that Mechanics' Institute. When the men surrendered, dropping weapons, hands up, the white mob murdered them anyway, right in the streets. Paul Dostie was holding a white flag when they shot him.

I expect no kind of justice here. I'm just another darky, hardly worth throwing away the life of one of their own, guilty or not.

So, we really only here on account of how loud Buford screamed when I cut him. Like a babe with the colic. They saw my clothes, shredded like I'd been clawed by a lion. And they saw Buford, too big around the shoulders and too rough around the hands to be a priest. The police grabbed Buford on the spot. We made the papers. That's why we here. Because of all the attention.

"That man at that table over there?" I ask.

"Yes, miss," Davidson, the attorney of the City of New Orleans, says. "Have you seen him afore?"

"The man over there who's ugly as sin?" Some of my folk up the gallery laugh again. But the men in the juror box are beet-faced.

"Miss Pittman, I must insist—"

I squint. "I never seen that man before in all my born life," I say. "I swear it." People all around the room gasp.

The judge bangs his gavel. Buford's lawyer with the round glasses stands.

"Your honor, I move for an immediate dismissal of the present matter."

Later, it's dark out. The bells of St. Louis Cathedral over Jackson Square ring out. This is how I know it's round midnight when Buford shows his face at the exit of the district jail. A policeman shoves him out. Buford dusts off his coat and starts toward the cathedral. But he won't make it. I doubt he was going to pray to the Lord anyhow. Don't matter none. My basket is full of baguettes and oranges for my young ones. And I have a knife. A long one, too. I use it for gutting sow. When I pull it out, it shakes like it's singing. Don't matter if Buford was going to pray. I'm his Lord tonight.

Bigsby

That's the way it was when I was younger. I never had a hard time getting a date—I'm not bragging. I'm not, I swear. Probably because I grew up with three sisters, y'know? The chicks always liked me. Black chicks, too. Man, if I went out, they'd give me the eye. You know women don't just look a guy they don't know in the face. Amirite? Yeah. I dated some. There was this one in college. I haven't thought about her in some time. Aisha. She got closer to me than most. By junior year, I was staying at her apartment more than in my own dorm. We got along well. Did everything together for a while. Picnics in City Park. Day trips to the beach in Biloxi. People would stare. At first, I thought it was because she was so good-looking. She had this shape. I mean not just her hips and stuff. Her face was heart shaped. And those eyes. We fizzled out.

That's right, then I met Samantha. Those redheads, bro! Dammit. Why you always got to drag that ghost out the closet? You want to know what happened with us, Kyle? I'll tell you what happened. Then don't ever bring her up again. This shit whiskey is giving me a headache. Order something better. Don't be so damned cheap. Samantha was perfect, and we fell in love quick. It wasn't just the usual things like compatibility and looks. She was ambitious. She wanted to make an empire with me. Her father was older and had this company that put video poker machines in all the bars. I know it don't sound like much, but do you know how many bars there are in New Orleans? That family was loaded, and she wanted to take over one day and keep expanding it.

One day, I came home to our condo downtown. She was my fiancée by then. We were considering a June wedding. We were talking about buying a house in Old Metairie, starting a family. Her parents would cover the cost of everything. They would have to. My family had nothing to contribute. I had less than nothing. That day, the condo was so quiet. I thought Samantha was out for a jog or maybe down at the coffee shop. But she was sitting on the bed holding some paper. Her face was blotchy. She looked terrible. She asked how I could lie to her the way I did. She threw the papers at me, but they fell on the floor. I'm thinking she's accusing me of running around on her, like she'd hired a PI or something. But I wasn't like that anymore. I picked up the papers.

It was one of those breakdowns from a company that checks your DNA. It wasn't her idea. She said her mother must have swabbed a cup I drank out of or something. I was furious. I mean, who does that, bro! I could've punched a hole in the wall. The percentages were highlighted. I had plenty of points on the European side of things like Irish and Italian, but it also said twenty-four percent sub-Saharan Africa. This was news to me, and that's what I told Samantha. She said she wasn't a bigot. But she had to think of her parents. What would she tell her friends? Her Nana? I moved out about a week later.

Yeah this better, Kyle. This real whiskey. No. I don't think that sheet was right. I think all that computerized mumbo jumbo is bullshit. I know my family tree. My great-grandparents were still alive when I was little. They had roots in Sicily. I know my heritage. Fuck! Get me another shot of this. Don't be cheap. Make it a double. Funny thing is, years later, I ran into Aisha at that festival they throw out in Ponchatoula. Yeah. The one with strawberries. And we kind of picked up where we left off. Eventually, one night I told her about those papers and she was all like, "I sho reckoned. You ain't got no pink in yo' skin. That's why you so fine." She didn't really talk like that. She was snooty—had gone and got herself an English PhD. Taught at a college. Spoke better than I do. A couple of times, I told her that sheet was wrong, but she just nodded. We didn't end up lasting that long the second time around. I couldn't have her loving me for something I'm not.

Rhinoceros

After midnight, Shaquann and Freddie pedal the stolen glowing tandem bike to Magnolia Stables, a place where horses snort and dream. Along the way, they dodge potholes and cars full of weed-smoking white boys. At the stable door, a jeweled surgical mask over her lower face, Shaquann's chest heaves and sweat collects at her brow. Freddie rubs her sweaty palms down the front of her jeans. There's an electronic lock on the stable door. Freddie takes it as a sign. Sometimes bad things give you a little warning first, like a stern librarian wagging a finger.

"We should go," Freddie says. "They might have cameras."

"So, what if they do, little girl?" Shaquann says. "What they gone see? You looking like a ghetto astronaut." Shaquann is joking, but Freddie can't disagree. Afraid of the virus in the air, she wears many layers of protection: a face shield, disposable gloves, and two masks—one medical grade and a cloth scarf one that covers her neck, mouth, and nose—to say nothing of her large glasses, steamed from breath.

Shaquann kicks the lock once, the hem of her yellow-flowered summer dress flaring on the humid air. Freddie told her to go all black, formfitting, hard to see, like herself. But Shaquann wasn't hearing it. She tossed her hair. *This exactly when you want to look good. When you making trouble.*

Freddie taps the stable door handle. "What do we do?"

"Didn't you pick up anything from me about how to take charge?" Shaquann asks. When Freddie doesn't move, Shaquann exhales in exaggerated frustration. "Fine. Watch and learn. The sooner we do this, the sooner we get to the protest."

"Too many people," Freddie says. She and Shaquann have been in a push-pull situation all day. The protesters have been down at Duncan Plaza every day this week despite the virus. But the thought of being in that crush of bodies, even masked and shielded, makes Freddie's skin prickle. She told Shaquann she wasn't going. But then again, she also told Shaquann she wasn't coming to the stable.

"Don't start that talk again." Shaquann disappears around the corner of the building and Freddie wonders if Shaquann hopped on the stolen bike and left. But she wouldn't. Breaking in for the people is her idea. "Come around."

Shaquann is standing by a large open portal halfway up the wall. She gestures with a flourish. "See? They locked the door but left a whole hole."

"How'd you know this would be open?"

"I didn't. That's the point. You ain't looking, you ain't finding."

"Are we really doing this?" Freddie asks.

Even masked, Freddie can tell she's smiling. "Is we alive, little boy?" Shaquann is playing with Freddie's pronouns again. Of course, she had told Shaquann first. In fact, she had only told Shaquann. It was Shaquann who inspired her to put her thoughts down in the journal. In her palm-sized, three-for-a-dollar notebook, Freddie debated whether to keep it to herself that she didn't need to be called *she*. She didn't need to be called *he* either. So *they* is what you want? Shaquann would later ask. But Freddie hadn't been sure about that either. She felt more and more lately that all of the words belonged to her. Having to choose felt unfair, like being made to leave several gifts because you already had one in your hand.

Freddie cups her hands, but Shaquann shakes her head. Freddie understands. Shaquann is taller. She must give Freddie the boost. With a quick move, Freddie is atop the portal.

Inside the stall, a horse stands, nose to the interior of the darkened building. The animal's tail flicks. Freddie goes to the stall door. The other horses are silent in their places. Their black eyes glisten like something from a painting. *The Night Mares,* Freddie thinks and chuckles at her easy pun. She has been near horses at Mardi Gras parades. The pungent, earthy smell of their bodies always surprises her. She hates the smell of her own sweat or of anything that gets sullied with funk or grime. But horses are the exception. Their scent makes her giddy. She wants to hug them all.

"Don't they sleep?" Shaquann asks.

"They dream on their feet," Freddie says. "But they're awake now."

"How you know these things, Fredericka?" It takes them a minute to get Shaquann onto the animal's back without a saddle. The creature is surly at first, this horse with the star on his forehead, but Shaquann isn't flustered. The latest report of a vicious attack on a trans woman in Mid-City lit something in Shaquann's brain that day. *We going out tonight.*

She sits sidesaddle and places the tiara she brought on her head. She has a thin, sparkling scepter, too, which she flourishes as if to say *Hurry, peasant.* Freddie takes a bunch of shots with her phone. It's not easy to see through the face shield, which is also fogging up. But the lighting is good enough, and the horse seems to like Shaquann. Woman and animal shift positions from left to right like they are posing on a fashion runway. Shaquann lifts her chin. "The camera loves us. Just like Jesus."

"Y'all look good," Freddie says, "but don't you think that's enough horsing around?"

"Hush, child, with your puns," Shaquann says. "We are not amused. You don't rush royalty."

After Shaquann climbs down, she reaches into her slouchy purse and feeds the horse baby carrots.

Freddie adjusts her shield, which is nearly opaque with mist, looking over surprised at Shaquann.

"You not the only one know how to Google horse care. I ain't ignorant—"

The sound of locks sliding out of position at the stable door they couldn't open. Hinges creaking. Shaquann and Freddie stare at each other. Shaquann motions for them to go for the portal. Freddie shakes her head. She has a vision of clambering up the side of the wall but slipping and knocking herself unconscious. She took Ls even in her imagination.

"Get down," Shaquann says. Freddie ducks into the corner next to the stall gate and presses her back against the wall. Shaquann crouches in the opposite corner, clutching a sandal in her hand, as though to boomerang it at whoever is approaching.

Footsteps thump closer. She feels like something small and furry curled inside a wall. A shotgun barrel, like an elephant's trunk, enters the stall first, bobbing back and forth slightly, seemingly to the bearer's heartbeat. The barrel is followed by the body of a white man in a thin T-shirt that reveals the shape of his gut. The man lowers the muzzle toward Shaquann. Freddie tries to will Shaquann to chill out. Not to do anything crazy. Not to say anything crazy. But Shaquann isn't even looking at her.

"You don't belong in here," the man says.

"Mister," Shaquann says, "you ain't got to tell me. I was just going home." She rises to one knee like she's about to stand. The man's pants pocket is overflowing with red and gold shotgun shells. The bulge looks like grapes.

"Don't move till I tell you to," he says, leering at her. "Why are you wearing a dress?"

"Because it's hot. Why are you wearing a kindergartner's T-shirt?"

Freddie's neck is hot. *Why Shaquann got to joke?* Freddie can barely inhale.

"Shut up!" Freddie says. Then clamps a hand over her own mouth.

"Who?" the man says, turning toward Freddie. "Oh!" Shaquann lunges shoulder first at the man's legs. He slams into the stall doorjamb, head knocking into the wood door. His legs are splayed out in front of him, his grip is loose around the shotgun, but still holds on. His free hand lifts up to check for blood on the back of his head. Freddie and Shaquann step over his legs and scurry out.

Shaquann's head is in Freddie's lap, as they sit on the curb outside of a pet groomer's on Magazine Street. Shaquann's long, storky legs are crossed into the street. Freddie absent-mindedly strokes Shaquann's hair. There's a wild part that won't lie down. Freddie and Shaquann don't have to rush because they're not expected in the places they live. Shaquann's mama is a night guard at a skyscraper, while her daddy does maintenance at a hotel. Freddie's mama works at a rich-people's nursing home by the river. It's where all the deaths in New Orleans started. Freddie's mama didn't want to spread the sickness—they said you could have it without knowing—so she slept most nights at the nursing home.

Shaquann takes a ham-and-cheese finger sandwich

from the aluminum foil on her flat stomach and pokes the triangle toward Freddie's mouth. Freddie had made the sandwiches for Shaquann because she likes watching her eat. She shakes her head. Shaquann eats the triangle and talks fullmouthed.

"You'll need your strength for the protest."

"I guess." Wispy clouds skid across the sky.

"Why you pouting?" Shaquann asks.

"I'm over going to that protest," Freddie says, "and all these stunts, too." When she says *stunts,* she is speaking of all the things they have been doing lately. Shaquann seems to think protest art and social progress go together like prayers and answered prayers. They put a black hood over the head of the John McDonogh statue last weekend. Before that, Shaquann spray-painted a black fist on the window of a building where rich old white men meet to divide spoils. Each time, Freddie and Shaquann had been observed, because New Orleans was a city where people were always out and watching other people, even during a pandemic. They didn't care about being watched. That made them take their time.

Shaquann rolls and sits upright. A row of bushes ring the front of the pet groomer's. The bush leaves rubbing together in the breeze sound like rain.

"You scared because of that guy at the stable," Shaquann says. "I knocked him on his butt. You know I look out for you."

This was true. Before the schools closed, Freddie was coming out of the first-floor boys' bathroom, her three-ring library club binder pressed to her ribs. She was wearing the uniform skirt she hated. The Catholic school policed what she wore on her body down to the millimeter. It was against the rules to wear pants, but she also got chastised if the skirt's hemline rose above her fingertips as if there were some golden zone of flesh revealing that pleased God. Freddie was adjusting her skirt when that skeevy cop, the officer, a brother, who was supposed to look out for suspicious intruders, called to her from the water fountain.

"You seem confused about a few things," he said with a grunt-laugh. The girls' bathroom was a single stall and always occupied by adult staff, so Freddie gravitated to the boys' bathroom when it was empty instead of trekking to the other girls' upstairs. But really who cared what bathroom she used? Who actually cared? The cop was doing elevator eyes. He started at her shoes. Scuffed Mary Janes. He stopped at her hair, which the prior night, after seeing too many depressing stories on Twitter—Black people filling the ICU wards of the city, second line dancers mobbed by the police, dead construction workers haunting a collapsed building—Freddie had buzzed down. It was liberating to move without elaborate braids weighing at her neck. She wondered what her mama would say next time she saw her. But the feeling of air across her shorn nape was a new kind of freedom.

"I think you should bring that hair back," the cop snickered, walking alongside her. He was stocky with a two-inch fro. His eyes, small and quick. He stuck out his arm to block her.

"Leave me alone." Freddie ducked under his arm and kept walking. She had moved from the hallway to the cafeteria area that branched off to the side. Assemblies were held there, but the tables where students ate and talked were empty. Everyone was in class.

"No need to get uptight, baby. I'm just here to help. I got a daughter, too. She seven." Freddie wanted to respond, wanted to say that she felt sorry for his daughter. But she didn't want to set him off. She strode away without slowing. "Hey, don't ignore me!" He grabbed her arm.

"Ow!" Freddie said.

"Oh hell no." It was Shaquann. Freddie knew of Shaquann because she was popular, a majorette for the band who spoke on MLK Day. But Shaquann was a senior and Freddie just an honors-student junior so they didn't interact. Shaquann wore bland khakis during school hours, but they couldn't stop her from pressing and curling her hair like Big Freedia.

"This ain't your business," the cop said.

"Listen. You don't put your hands on anyone's child in my school." Shaquann was nudging the cop's shoulder.

"Now hold on," the cop said.

"You better step, little man, or I'll have you in pedophile prison with no shoestrings." The cop looked around and left.

"Are you okay?" Shaquann asked. Freddie was shaking, biting her lip. "That was good. You stood up for yourself good."

"I didn't do anything," Freddie said. "I don't do anything."

A bus with people in work clothes passes the pet groomer's. Freddie edits one of Shaquann's photo and uploads it. Immediately, the notifications spill in. And they should— Freddie is proud of the way she doctored the ambient light. Shaquann's masked face is blurred, but haloed, light beams spreading out behind her. Freddie scribbled and shaded letters below and behind the horse: *Blk Trns Lvs Mttr*. The words look like they're in the stall with Shaquann. The post is already up to a thousand likes within a few minutes on their anonymous Instagram account.

"We need to show people we're serious."

"Do we really?" Freddie says. "I just want to live."

"That's the whole point," Shaquann says. "Anyway." Shaquann texts somebody on her phone. "I'm getting a ride."

"Why don't we just ride our bike?"

"I'm through exerting myself on the rig. I need to save something for the protest."

"But I don't want to—"

"Lookah," Shaquann says. "Unless you want to walk again, you're coming with me."

The light ring along the bike's front rim partly obscures the tire. But Freddie sees the rubber pooling on the concrete. Freddie had complained about all the walking around town during their prior stunts. She'd worn a corrective shoe when she was younger, but her right foot still wasn't quite like the other, and it hurt most of the time. Earlier that night, Shaquann had shown up with the two-seater bike, likely borrowed from one of the French Quarter vendors,

Freddie assumed. Riding it with Shaquann in front of her felt like endlessly diving into a cool, clean pool.

Within fifteen minutes, a gray SUV with tinted windows pulls up to the curb. The SUV has a low hood and is highly polished with chunky, muscular tires. The vehicle looks like a thick-skinned animal about to charge.

Two boys get out. No. Not boys. Men. One of them wears a tank top and shorts. He has a round, childlike face and skinny legs but the tattooed, buff arms of a circus performer who walks on his hands. The other man is light-skinned in a crisp, collared shirt. He has a soft mouth that suggests sucking lemons.

Freddie pulls Shaquann aside.

"Uh-uh," Freddie whispers. "I ain't going with those dudes. They grown!"

"I'm grown, too," Shaquann also whispers. "I'm out of high school. Even if I had to get my diploma in the mail." All the seniors graduated during a thirty-minute online ceremony Freddie watched while also viewing videos of a new challenge where young people went into their parents' bedrooms and planked just before sunrise. The punch line was to catch their parents' reactions when they found their child seemingly deceased.

"They not even wearing masks," Freddie says.

"I ain't crazy. They clean. They get tested bout every day for work. Look, that's one of my boos. He the one bought me this purse."

"You don't need a sugar daddy to buy you a purse."

"You ain't never had nobody be nice to you?" Shaquann

45

says it more like a statement than a question. Freddie sinks back into herself and stares at Shaquann, who is already looking over Freddie's shoulder.

"We good?" the buff one asks, leaning against the fender. Shaquann walks over and takes his hand.

"Freddie, this my friend, Rocky. He's a deputy at the parish prison. And this his cousin, Bee." Bee throws a languid peace sign.

"That bike won't fit in my ride, and I ain't got no rack." Rocky's chewing a gingerroot. It pokes out the side of his mouth.

Shaquann looks at the bike. Freddie thinks Shaquann will say they need to find a way.

"I ain't sweating that, baby," Shaquann says. "It wasn't even mine."

Rocky opens the front passenger door and gives Shaquann a hand into the SUV. Once everyone is inside, they take off. Freddie admits to herself that the air-conditioned interior is a relief after hours in the dank hotness of New Orleans in summer. But the SUV is musty. It's a creeping smell that unfolds in waves, sweat, garbage, mold. They turn onto St. Charles Avenue. A streetcar shadows them like a crocodile along a shoreline.

"Thank you for the ride," Freddie says.

"You welcome," Rocky says. He pats the dashboard. "This my baby. Just upgraded the seats. That's Corinthian leather you're sitting on." Freddie touches the seat. It feels like skin.

"Got a 460 under the hood," Rocky says.

"What's a 460?" Freddie asks. Rocky laughs.

"Y'all really trying to go to this protest thing?" Rocky says. "For what?"

"People tired of all the bullshit," Shaquann says. "All this brutality. We trying to get rights up in here. Rights for trans people. Rights for queer people. Rights for Black people."

"Mostly white folk out there what I heard." Bee is holding his phone, his thumb streaking across the screen like a windshield wiper on the high-speed setting. "They going to try to cross the bridge."

"Well, I ain't feeling it," Rocky says. "But I know Shaq's got to go. She's all into that white meat."

"Boy, you play too much." Shaquann play-slaps Rocky's shoulder. He smiles at her. When they stop at a light, Rocky tongue-kisses Shaquann.

"I'm not going to it," Freddie says. "That sounds like a mess."

"Your friend got sense. They probably gonna be shooting people."

"Nobody ain't doing all that," Shaquann says. "It'll be peaceful."

"Some of this about that girl who got trampled last night? I know all about that. My dude at the corner store said it was mistaken identity. The guys thought she was a girl girl."

"What that even mean?" Shaquann asks. The video—videos—were all over and Freddie didn't want to watch, but once Freddie started watching last night, she couldn't turn away. The way the men punched and grabbed the woman as if to stun and dismantle. They pulled her hair, yanked her clothes, grabbed her earrings, snatched her purse, all while onlookers recorded and *ooo*'ed.

"People need to know what they working with," Rocky says. "Those girls should wear armbands or something."

"You being so rude right now," Shaquann says.

Freddie leans forward in her seat. She grabs the back of Rocky's headrest for balance even as her seatbelt's tension pulls at her waist. "If someone is freaked out about another person's body that gives them the right to attack them?"

"It wasn't even personal. It was a reaction, is what I'm saying. Like slapping a mosquito on your arm."

"That's sick, Rocky," Shaquann says. She twists her upper body around to address Bee. "What do you think?"

Bee glances up from his phone and watches Rocky for a moment. "I don't know. You never know how someone gonna come at you, especially round here. You might be chilling and then they about to run right over you."

Shaquann sits straight in her seat. "So, you would have done me like that if I wasn't what you expected? Would have had me looking like I got beat with a bat?"

"Nah, baby." Rocky places a hand on Shaquann's leg. "You know I don't see you that way. You just you." He runs his hand up her thigh.

Shaquann smacks her lips. Outside the SUV, the shadowed mansions give way to bright storefronts where ball gowns hang and advertisements for cellphones promise incredible speed.

"That kind of thing happens every day," Bee says.

"What's that?" Rocky asks.

"People getting fed up with the situation they in." Bee turns on the light over his head. Suddenly, the reflection of his face appears in the window. As though he wants to see himself while he talks. "Remember Ms. Cola?"

"At the place where they pay your electric light bill?" Rocky says.

"You mean, People's Community Action?" Shaquann says.

"Right," Bee says. Freddie's mama had brought her there several times over the years. It was a warehouse full of desks and lines of people asking for what their jobs didn't pay enough to provide. A lake of people in hats, shower caps, or work overalls. Freddie's mama brought her last time for a school uniform voucher. Freddie felt somehow that she was in two places at once. PCA where the voices of people like hers echoed off the aluminum ceiling and Ellis Island where immigrants once waited for whatever justice the land might provide.

"I know her," Shaquann says. "She has them cat-eye glasses."

"My gramma friend," Bee says. "She worked there for thirty years. Then about a month ago before all this mess with the virus started, she just got up from her desk and said she had a vision. She was getting a train ticket to Chicago where things ain't so crazy."

"How it's less crazy there?" Rocky asks.

"I mean she used to sit behind that desk," Bee says.

"Paying people's bills day in, day out. And she bounced without even turning her computer off because of something she didn't even see with her eyes. See you later. I'm gone. *Poof.*"

"What was her vision?" Freddie asks.

"Something about singing on a field of grass on a hill."

"Child, they ain't got no grassy hills in Chicago," Shaquann says.

"How would you even know?" Rocky lowers his rearview mirror to get a view of Bee. "Bee's Ma used to have visions before they put her away."

"Don't trip, bruh." Bee lowers his gaze back to his phone.

"Maybe that lady at Community Action had family in Illinois," Freddie says, changing topics.

The SUV rounds the traffic circle that borders downtown. Freddie presses her face shield to the window and follows the line of the concrete plinth upward to the empty pedestal. Once a Confederate statue stood there until they brought in a crane, looped a noose around the idol, and ripped it off. At the gas station, a group of men made jerky movements with their hands as if in a rap battle. Freddie blew to leave condensation on the glass of the SUV, but it just fogged her face shield again.

"What you is anyway?" Rocky asks. He's angled the mirror to watch her now.

"What?"

"I mean you got all the junk on. You might be a woman, an undocumented immigrant, a Russian hacker. I can't even tell. Makes me nervous."

"Don't be rude, Rocky, baby," Shaquann says.

"Shaq said you're in a 'transitional phase.'" Rocky laughs.

"I said Freddie is exploring her identity."

"What? Like you lost it on the bus?" Bee asks.

"How you not know who you are?" Rocky says.

"Excuse me," Freddie says, "I need to get out." The SUV was in slow traffic. Freddie pulled the door handle, but it was child locked.

"Hey, I was just playing," Rocky says, the gingerroot sliding in and out of the corner of his mouth.

Shaquann glances back at Freddie. There's a look of uncertainty in Shaquann's eye.

"Chill out, girl," Shaquann says.

Freddie unbuckles her seatbelt. She moves to the lip of the bench seat. She leans into the space between Shaquann and Rocky.

"I'm giving you five seconds to stop, unlock this door, and let me out."

Rocky stops the SUV in front of an office building. He gets out and pulls her door open, all the while shaking his head.

"You being crazy," Shaquann says.

"You can stay," Freddie says. Even as the SUV pulls away, Freddie can hear Shaquann calling after her as though from the far side of a river.

Freddie jogs several blocks. She comes to a large, dark-ened plate-glass window and sees her reflection. The black skinny jeans. The formless black T-shirt. The layers of protection around her head. The phrase *armored shadow* flits through her mind. She pulls off the face shield and both masks. Holding them in either hand, she leans forward, hands on knees, breathing deeply. She swings at her reflection and the face shield slams off the glass. The shield skitters across the ground. She kicks it.

A noise draws her attention back down the block. The gray SUV screeches at the intersection and the front passenger door pops open. Shaquann gets out. She slams the door. The tinted rear passenger rolls down. Bee dumps the contents of Shaquann's purse onto the ground.

"This my ride!" Rocky says. The SUV's engine roars, but the vehicle stays in place.

Freddie runs to Shaquann. Shaquann's cheeks are wet, her face contorted.

"Come here." Freddie hugs Shaquann and wipes her cheek with her sleeve.

"They can go to hell," Shaquann says. "I'm sorry."

"I know." Freddie takes her hand.

"You know," Shaquann says. "Look at you." They both laugh.

Freddie notices the SUV hasn't moved from where it stopped a few yards away, exhaust spitting from the tailpipe. She sees the aggressive curves of the fenders and bumpers. The chunky, muscular tires. The flat planes of the door panels polished to a mirror sheen, waiting to be shattered.

Ghetto University

You would think a black man with two advanced degrees, who had once lectured at the Sorbonne, who shook hands with Noam Chomsky and Shirin Ebadi, who prefers Enya to Kanye West, and who will never willingly watch a Tyler Perry film, would not spend his evenings mugging tourists in the French Quarter. And you would be wrong.

For instance, take this couple ahead of me. It's early evening, and they're strolling toward that awful tourist trap, Café Du Monde. I peg them for Midwesterners, probably Minnesotans, with their button-down shirts and matching mom jeans. They're distracted by an argument, easy prey for me. On earlier nights like this one, back before the budget cuts that led to my termination from the university, I would have politely greeted this couple, even cheerfully so.

"I don't want no trouble," I say, tugging my sweatshirt

hood forward. With my black medical-grade mask, I imagine I look suitably intimidating. But I'm using the mask for an off-label use. It's a holdover from many months ago when the pandemic began.

"Please don't shoot us," the woman says instantly.

"Nobody has got to get shot," I say. "You know what to do." I throw in a "whitey" for effect, even though I know that lukewarm racial epithet hasn't been popular since the 1970s, but how exactly does one insult white people? Hey, Casper? Fork it over, paleface? There simply isn't a word equivalent to the N-bomb when you're trying to make Caucasians feel uncomfortable, unless you count the most terrifying noun, my skin.

My take from the encounter is modest but satisfying. A couple hundred dollars and passes to a reenactment of the 1811 German Coast Uprising. I keep the cash and toss the passes. I'm in the middle of my own uprising. I don't need to observe one.

Back home, my wife, Dell, preps her face at the dresser mirror. She's a chemist for one of the oil companies and often takes the graveyard shift, monitoring that certain necrotizing chemicals don't leap from their containers and dive into the water table. Her recent attention to cosmetics is odd to say the least, since for most of our marriage she cared little about fashion, but who can account for the mercurial whims of women? I do hope she's not cheating on me.

Yes, I've been in a snippy mood, and, sure, I've put on a few pounds over the years, but my recent nocturnal activities combined with a reduction in my consumption of HoHos has led to promising gains, or, rather, losses.

"How did you do today, darling?" she asks. I show her my booty—the money, that is. "That's it?" She pinches her nose, that unhappy, nervous tic of hers. "For the whole day? Seriously, James. If things weren't going so well at the lab, we'd already be out on the street, homeless and shaking a cup. When are you going to find real work?"

Dell doesn't know what I've been doing. I spent the first week of my disenfranchisement inquiring at other local institutions of higher learning, even the vocational schools. Yet, as you can imagine, a city with a 30 percent illiteracy rate isn't exactly aching to employ a professor of English who specializes in the verse of Alexander Pushkin.

Since my leads dried up, I've been tutoring trust-fund babies on how to ace their college admission essays. Or so Dell thinks. I actually tried the tutoring madness once. It was mostly discouraging. My pupil was the daughter of a wealthy uptowner, the owner of a plantation turned resort west of the city. I couldn't disabuse that girl of the notion that the reading of literature was not, *like, a total waste of time and why can't I just, like, draw them a picture?*

"Everybody likes pictures, right, instructor?" she asked, not wearing a mask because her father told her the pandemic was a political hoax.

"Professor," I said, straightening my posture.

"Like, whatever. All I'm saying is people get more out of art and music than some words on a page."

Dell brushes her eyebrows. She's always brushing her eyebrows these days. No one's eyebrows in the history of the world have been subjected to more rigorous brushing than hers. "I know you think online teaching is beneath you—"

"I'm not doing that," I say. "It's hard enough to help students learn while they're sexting each other in the classroom. How much more difficult will it be when they have Big Bootied Bitches open in the web browser next to mine?" My whole body quivers. Dell is right, of course. We have no savings, evictions are allowed again, and the rent is weeks overdue. The landlord crammed a crude letter through the mail slot earlier today. The missive couldn't have been less eloquent if it were scribbled in crayon. How he managed to spell "eviction" properly I'll never know. He wants this month's and next month's rent by tomorrow morning.

Dell places a hand on my cheek and frowns. "Oh, darling," she says, "you look tired. There's mac and cheese in the oven. Get some sleep. Bye." Then she's gone. I can't remember the last time I saw her smile.

After consuming copious chunks of Dell's ambrosia, I return to the streets. This is a good time of year for mugging. The convention trade is only half as good as it used to be, but the discount rates have drawn out bargain-hunting organizations. Last Wednesday, the World Commission on Peace stopped by. Next week, the NRA. Tonight? The International Association of Lepidopterists, even though there are virtually no interesting butterflies in New Orleans. I wear a butterfly brooch on my hoodie to blend in. The brooch is somewhat in the shape of a blue morpho. The silhouette is correct, but the spots are all wrong.

Tourists commit all the right sins for my purposes: gluttony, sloth, and pride. They spend their days devouring clichés: salty gumbo, po'boy sandwiches with crusty exteriors and soft, chewy interiors, and sweet, powdery beignets. By evening, they're stuffed to their medullas. Lounging on a bench in Jackson Square, their bellies distended, they say *Wouldn't it be nice if we went to see the plaque where the slave auction block used to be? It'll be a blast. Jack and Lydia were here, and they didn't get to see it. We could post pictures on social media and rub their noses in our good fortune.* And then the tourists wander off without a map.

New Orleans is like a brick. You pour water on it and there's no telling where the rivulets will run. When tourists trickle through our neighborhoods, they puddle in places they would have done well to avoid.

Like this courtyard, where, spiderlike, I'm hanging out behind a stand of poplar trees. A French family has fallen onto my web, four of them this time, a disgruntled man, a cigarette-sucking woman, a teen girl on a cellphone, and a boy in a fleur-de-lis baseball cap, rakishly tugged sideways. I know what you're thinking. He's not going to mug a family with kids.

But you see, it's already done. A simple shuffle into their path with the grace of Muhammad Ali in his prime.

"Papa," the boy says, misinterpreting our tableau. *"Le rappeur! Le rappeur! C'est MC Solaar!"* I quickly clear up the confusion.

Next thing, I've acquired two new cellphones, a wad of euros, which I'll convert shortly, and the most delightful Nicholas of Myra pendant, the jolly old saint of pawnbrokers and thieves. *Quelle chance!*

Guilt? I feel none for three reasons. First, although my prey thinks otherwise, I'm unarmed. No gun. No knife. No club. If anything, I have only a face and body that are, in a sense, weaponized. And there's nothing illegal about people giving me currency, portable electronics, or heirloom jewelry of their own free will. I've never once asked my patrons for a dime. I'm just a very aggressive beggar, if one really considers it.

I discovered the generosity of people years before I had need of this knowledge. In my teaching career, I favored cashmere vests and tweed coats. Yes, I know. It's stereotypical, but much of the reason I became a professor in the first place was so that I could look like a professor. Wear the sophistication of one. I may have even worn a bow tie on occasion.

Once, I spilled a cup of heavily creamed Darjeeling, ruining my favorite ensemble, klutz that I am. I stripped in my office and would have had to go home to change if not for the oversized T-shirt some long-forgotten freshman had left behind during advising hours. I wore the T-shirt to the restroom. There was a janitor, I don't recall his name, to which I often gave the briefest wave on my way to lecture. I caught him glaring at me.

"Who are you?" he said.

"What?"

"Clean yourself somewhere else," he said. "We don't allow no homeless people to hang up in this building."

"Now, wait a second—" But the poor guy dropped his mop and left. In the hall, I watched him retreat in search of the campus police. A simple change of clothes had thrown me all the way down the ladder of my achievements.

Second, I'm doing my benefactors a valuable service. How so? Ever had a health scare? A near-fatal car accident? Knowledge that a plane crashed and you survived only because you missed your flight? Invariably, I imagine, my supporters are much happier for having been graced by my presence. That arguing Norwegian American couple can return to Minnesota with a fresh appreciation for their general good fortune. And that francophone family now understands the primacy of their kinship. Having not died together, perhaps they will live together. All thanks to *moi*.

Last? I deserve my take. Consider my profits reparations for each time some Becky or Karen crossed the street to avoid my path just as I greeted them. I regift that horror to you, my lovely brunette friends.

It's a red-letter evening. I've encountered no less than five separate groups since leaving home. I've been so effective that I notice an increased police presence in the Quarter. Blue shirts. Mounted patrolman. Ridiculously obvious undercover cops in heavily starched muscle shirts. Honestly, who starches a muscle shirt?

As I stroll past a honky-tonk, I see a police sketch on the television. An approximation of my face. My heart skips a beat, but then I remember that anonymity is part of my power. How do my marks describe me? *Well, he was tall. He wore a mask. And, um, he was really dark. No. Darker.* Good luck finding me.

On Barracks Street, the air smells of raspberry daiquiris and cigar smoke. Low, puffy clouds crawl southward. This is the quiet end of the Quarter, where magnolia blooms droop over the edges of flower boxes like partygoers who've had too much to drink. It's getting pretty late when I spot a lone man ambling along. An overstuffed camera bag rhythmically bounces against the man's side. His wallet winks at me from a back pocket. The man, in a flimsy surgeon's mask, makes my mouth water. In this moment, I know how the king of the jungle feels when, on the grasslands of the Serengeti, he spots a hapless zebra foal, separated from his harem. This will be an easy one.

Yet, the man advances at a remarkably brisk pace. His legs hardly seem to move at all, but he's outdistancing me. Have I been spotted? Is he running for help? I have to jog to catch up with him, and I do. I need only make him aware of my presence to end this transaction, but just as I come within striking distance moonlight illuminates the high-cheeked plane of his face. Oh, my goodness, he's black.

This situation has never presented itself before. On the one hand, he's clearly a tourist like all the others. On the other hand, it seems patently unfair to subject one of my own kind to such rough handling. When I say *my own kind*, I don't speak necessarily of his skin color, although to be perfectly honest that is a factor. But note the thick glasses, the stiffness of his gait, the comically tight high waters. In other words, this man is part of my tribe. He's a bona fide nerd.

Will my powers even work on someone so like myself, my blameless twin? Or will we cancel each other out in a burst of vapor, matter and antimatter dissolved to nothing? What kind of idiot wanders through the Quarter at such a late hour with such nonchalance, no self-awareness at all? Doesn't he realize that bad things happen to people who don't exercise common sense? He must learn to take better care of himself before something truly terrible happens. Despite my current employment status, I know that I'm an excellent teacher. I draw my hood forward and ready myself for the lesson.

"Hold it right there." Someone taps my shoulder from behind. My solicitor is a policeman wearing an N95 respirator. He pulls a horse by the reins. I back away.

"I said, 'Stop.'" The policeman places a hand on his hip, near his revolver. "I need to ask you a few questions." The horse bobs his head and snorts.

I run.

I hear the Mountie grunt onto his horse and, next, the sound of horseshoes against cobblestone. I sprint toward the still underpopulated, but not empty, heart of the Quarter. Neon signs glow in the distance. They're too far away to read, but I know what they advertise: sex, booze, violence. And if I make it that far, I may lose my assailant in the morass of pleasure-seeking tourists, securing my freedom. Feet don't fail me now.

As I sprint past a produce cart, I yank the bedsheet from it, a sheet the proprietor apparently hoped would protect his stock from prying eyes. But my plan is foiled because the cart is empty. I hoped the cart was full of apples. I hoped that apples would spill across the street like in one of those ludicrous action movies. I hoped the applelanche would cause my overseer to lose his balance and tumble to the ground. But I hoped wrong.

The horseman gains on me. I jump onto the sidewalk and bump past a pair of men peeing on the steps of the shabby old cathedral. The horseman follows me onto the sidewalk. My chest pounds. My temples thump. I won't be able go much farther before I collapse from total exhaustion. Out of options, I fling the white sheet into the air.

Buoyed on a breeze, the sheet snags my horseman's body, robing him in spotless cotton. The horseman's momentum carries him past me, as he grapples with his ghost. The hairs on the back of my neck stand up.

Depleted, but triumphant, I turn onto a side street and promptly trip on a hole in the sidewalk, twisting my ankle. Broken pavement: my tax dollars hard at work. In no time, I hear my hooded pursuer approaching from around the bend. Soon, I'll be a prisoner.

"Darling?" I'm pulled to my feet and into a narrow, fenced alley. I lean against a rugged brick wall. It takes me forever to catch my breath.

My savior is a sex worker, one of the countless women who unselfconsciously peddle their cupcakes and cookies at fire-sale prices. My heart aches for the desperate person who would look for street love at a time like this. The woman wears an ill-fitting blond wig and enough eye shadow to win *RuPaul's Drag Race,* but this woman is achingly familiar. She pulls off the shield that had been covering her face.

"Dell?" I ask. "What are you doing here dressed like that?"

"Me?" She pushes my hoodie back and wipes sweat from my forehead with a soft towel she takes from her pocket. "You're the one wearing a hoodie and jeans in the French Quarter. You hate hoodies. You hate jeans. You hate the French Quarter. James, you have a lot of explaining to do."

We tell each other the truth. Her end of it is that the oil company lost a government subsidy. In retaliation, they laid off the youngest, blackest, and, in this case, most female of their employees.

"So, you've been selling yourself?" I ask.

"Not in the traditional sense. No." She explains that she never has sex with the men or even undresses. To the contrary, she merely escorts them to a room, quickly dons a gas mask with a portable ventilator—like the face shield, borrowed equipment from her old job—and knocks her quarry out with a puff of neurogenic general anesthetic. You know, sleeping gas.

"I know what *neurogenic* means," I say.

"Actually"—she removes her wig—"it's more of a trihalomethane solution of my own synthesis. Perfectly safe and very effective—"

I place a finger over her lip.

"You did all of this," I ask, "to keep us from getting kicked out?"

Dell pulls a stack of crisp bills from her very large patent pleather purse. I unfurl my crumpled catch.

Dell counts the gathered money. We're close to our goal. She smiles.

"How did you know it was me you were saving?" I ask.

"What a preposterous question, darling," she says. "I'd know you anywhere."

Horse hooves tromp near the alley entrance. I motion for Dell to get behind me and wait in the shadows. If the horseman is back, I'll give myself up rather than let us both be arrested. I wouldn't want her to wind up in confinement with people like us.

I peek through the wooden fence slats, but don't find my pursuer. A horse-drawn carriage rolls past, but no sightseers warm its benches. My bedsheet drags behind, a carcass black with the grime of my city.

Dell and I squeeze out of the alley, her hand in mine. Sirens wail from the direction of the river, and blueberry lights flash across nearby rooftops. No doubt the horseman called reinforcements. Best to skedaddle while we can.

We altered our appearances as best we could. I trashed my hoodie in favor of the cream-colored polo shirt beneath. She stowed the wig and covered her mostly see-through costume with a wrinkled three-quarter-sleeve dress that had been wedged inside her bag. We look more or less like ourselves—a well-educated couple closing out an uneventful night on the town—or at least a harried approximation thereof.

We make the northern edge of the Quarter in no time, especially impressive as Dell wears platform heels, which she commands without incident. I've only known her to wear low heels. Who is this woman? I'm hardly one to buy into patriarchal notions of feminine scrumptiousness, but the heels create quiet a spectacle of her long legs. I do think I'll lobby for her to keep the heels once we put this strange business behind us.

We cross Basin Street, a tranquil lane where defunct railroad lines are still visible, northbound tracks breaching the pavement like metallic tree roots. A police helicopter, its searchlight a probing finger, slides into the area we just left. Dell clutches my hand. We trot even faster.

"Let's stop here," Dell says. "My feet are dead." We remove our face coverings. She sits on a bench next to a parking lot.

"Fine," I say. "Where is the car anyway?"

"The car?" She reaches into her bag, swapping the heels for flats.

"Yes. Our car." We own a jalopy. Both of us are terrified of debt, so we kept the car her parents gifted us when we married. It's antique, an egg-shaped electric-gas hybrid with leaky door seals, but it's ours.

"Why didn't you tell me that you'd resorted to psychological mugging?"

"Me?" I say. "Why didn't you tell me you were performing a Black Widow routine?"

"James Young, don't you dare change the subject. Caginess doesn't suit you."

I was going to object, but instead I grab her hands and hold them.

"I wanted to tell you everything but—it's just that you're such a good woman. You're so brilliant and beautiful and hardworking and beautiful. Sometimes I feel like I don't measure up. I wanted to get this one thing right for you."

Dell reaches over and grabs my chin. I lean into her and kiss her delicate lips. We pull apart. My mouth is hot, as if Cupid whacked me across my face with his bow.

"About the car," she says. "I sold it."

"You what?" I pull away.

"Earlier this evening. You see, I only stole from the one man I mentioned."

"But I've noticed you doing your face up for weeks."

"That was just preparation. You know I'm a planner, darling. I wanted to perfect my look. But frankly the idea of doing that more than once is terrifying."

A young, maskless couple saunters our way. It's clear that they've had too much to drink as they stumble like nectar-drunk honeybees. Sometimes life throws you an undeserved bone. Yes, I'm ready to put my unsavory enterprise in the rearview, but our rent remains due in just a few hours, and we're still short of our goal.

"How much more did you say we still need?" I ask. She tells me and does a double take from me to the couple who are getting quite close. They're a good-looking twosome in scarves, tall and towheaded like models in a Swedish travel brochure.

"Oh no, darling," Dell says. "No more. We're not doing that." The couple walks by. I don't want them to get away.

I grab Dell's upper arm. "We don't have a choice."

"Who does?" the woman of the couple asks.

Nestled in the folds of the man's cozy peacoat, the dark nub of a gun muzzle aims at my stomach. We're about to get mugged.

" 'O dreams, my dreams, where is your sweetness?' " I say, under my breath.

"This is no time for Pushkin," Dell says.

"We don't want no trouble, O. J.," the blond woman says.

Downrange, helicopter blades echo through the alleys and courtyards of the Quarter. Above, clouds collide and intermix, inkblots for my analysis, a purling moth, waltzing lovers, a beast with no name. Dell and I raise our hands in surrender.

Token

Get to the office by six A.M. each morning; never leave before sunset; wear a suit and tie even on Fridays; rock a bow tie and wear nonprescription glasses so they believe you have a brain; speak only when spoken to, but be sure to respond because the last thing you want to be is a quiet one: they fear the quiet ones; when you look in the mirror, be sure to see only a sliver of yourself; keep your car washed and your shoes mirror-shiny; be mocha-skinned, be walnut, be milk chocolate; let them consume you, and wipe their mouths with dirty linen, but don't associate with the Negros who work around the building: the security guards in their pressed-white short-sleeved shirts, the baggy-pants-wearing maintenance workers, the errand boys and food deliverers; don't let them connect you to any of those who look like you, because one of you is desirable, but more than one of you is a rebellion; never talk about Confederate monuments, police shootings, or protests; when you look in the mirror never find more than a drop of yourself; if you want to sell out, sell out smart; *but I'm not a sellout so much as a double agent;* this is how you drive to work; this is how you place your hands at two and ten o'clock; this is how you erect perfect posture in the elevator; this is how you greet your betters, which is everyone with white skin; you eat lunch at your desk, but always with the door closed; if they see you bite a hamburger or shovel fries into your pink mouth, they will have visions of savages with nose rings; they can wear nose rings, you cannot; never eat fried chicken on a workday because they will smell it on your smile; this is how you smile at your boss who called you soulful; this is how you smile at the descendant of the man who said *Segregation now, segregation forever;* this is how you smile when they call you by the name of another Black person; always go to the bathroom stall and always shut the door; never get caught next to one of the men at a urinal; they won't look past the divider at what you hold, but they will wonder about what you hold and whether it belongs to a person or an animal; they may look for a tail and you too will wonder even with your firsthand knowledge; when you look in the mirror, find a mask, always a mask; don't talk to the other people who wear suits and look like you; they can look like you, but like the white people better; don't play golf; your name is not Tyler, and you are not white; but if you must play golf do not agree to caddy and do not beat your betters; comfort them with cheerful conversation; tell all who will listen how grateful and lucky you are to be on the team;

this is how you appear to be twice the man you are; this is how you make hand motions that soothe; this is how you take a blow beneath your belt and fall to the parched earth; this is how you stay down and laugh it off; this is how you get up and let them pat your skull.

The Pie Man

The Pie Man tells Baby that a man has got to grab his own future for his own self. The City of New Orleans pays good to work disaster cleanup, and Baby would do well to cash in before all the money gets carted off. A lot more sensible, the Pie Man says, than running around punching on Spanish dudes. The Pie Man walks across the living room in his chef's jacket. He plops down on the couch, making himself at home. The walls have been stripped naked to the studs. Baby doesn't know which way his future is, but he's damn sure it's got nothing to do with scooping mold out of some abandoned school.

Baby sits at the plastic folding table in white briefs and a tank top, fingering the dry skin around his bulky plastic ankle bracelet. He plucks a Vienna sausage from its tin and tosses the wiener in his mouth. Baby eyes the Pie Man. The Pie Man doesn't seem to get that he has no claim on this place or anyone in it. Baby may be only fourteen, but this is his house. He's the man here.

The Pie Man's eyes are red. He kneads his face with both hands and looks around like he doesn't remember why he's there. Sauced out of his mind before noon. Probably spent the night with the winos back in Gert Town.

Baby's mama doesn't notice because she's too busy flapping around the room. As she gathers her things for the daycare center, she keeps clucking at him about making the right choices in life.

She's on Baby because a Latino day-jobber got jumped outside the package liquor last night, the latest in a string of Black on Brown beatdowns in retaliation for what happened to Baby's boy, Chaney. Baby's mama thinks Baby is part of the jump squad. He's not. Yet. He doesn't tell her this. If she and everyone else think he's in on the attacks, it beats the alternative.

Baby's mama checks her hair in a handheld mirror before placing the mirror on the table he's sitting at. It doubles as her dresser, like the couch doubles as her bed. Baby sleeps on the floor in his fleece blanket, wrapped up tight as a papoose. A portable stovetop makes the bathroom their kitchen. All their real stuff was destroyed in the flood from the levee breach after Hurricane Katrina passed nearly three years ago. They live in the front half of the house since the back is sealed off with blue tarp to keep the fungus odor out. It doesn't work. Everything smells like old people's feet to Baby.

Sanchez, the carpenter Baby used to gopher for, shot

Chaney in cold blood, but the police called it self-defense—
as if Chaney's back had a chance against Sanchez's .38.
Sanchez and the rest of the Latinos are afraid to work in
Baby's neighborhood. If they do work in his neighborhood,
they bring their guns, and sometimes use them. Baby's
mama still needed work done after Sanchez stopped coming around. She called the Pie Man, who worked sometimes with Baby and Sanchez, in to odd-job their Marengo
Street home three months ago because she can't afford a
contractor with papers or real tools.

One day when Baby came home from school, he found
the Pie Man's duffel of clothes on the rental sofa in the living room. The Pie Man been around for days, sizing up
what house repairs needed to be done. But Baby spotted
shaving cream in the bag, which was too much.

"What's this?" Baby asked, rubbing his own chin.

"He's going to help us get this place back together,"
Baby's mama said.

"No. I mean we can't just have some strange dude
sleeping here."

"You know he's not a stranger."

"He's lounging in my spot. That's where I lay my head."

"He sleeps in his van. Besides, you know he's your
father." Baby's mama had said this before. She told Baby
versions of her and the Pie Man's time in high school
together. They were senior superlatives, Cutest Couple. But
Baby tuned out whenever she started talking about his dad,
which he thought was something you proved not said.

"If he my daddy, where he been at all this time?"

"He's always been in your life, boy. Some people are more around than others. Who do you think paid for those sneakers you're wearing?"

Baby didn't like the idea of the drunk lurking around putting his fingers wherever he wanted. He chose to be outside of Baby's life. That was where he belonged. Baby pulled off his sneakers and threw them at the front door.

"Pick them up," Baby's mama said.

"Tell him to pick them up!" Baby said.

Chin on the table, eyes clamped shut, Baby realizes the Pie Man and his mama have been jabbering at him the whole time. He doesn't care and instead wonders what they were like when they met each other. During the time of Public Enemy and parachute pants. Back when the Pie Man's uneven flat-top fade was still in style.

They have a similar way of phoning in their rants. No commitment. They talk at him like they're being watched. As if they'll get in big trouble for failing to pay the right amount of lip service.

The Pie Man tells Baby he ought to respect his mama, man, because that's the least she deserves for bringing him into this unbalanced world, and if Baby's going to keep driving her every which way like he's been doing, then Baby ain't no kind of man. The whole issue could be that Baby's not thinking, says the Pie Man, but he can start anytime now. He tells Baby to sit up and pay attention. Because he doesn't know the Pie Man well, Baby does as he's told. The Pie Man could be crazy or something, like Baby's friend Touché.

"What, am I supposed to call you Pops or something?" Baby nudges his skateboard under the table with his bare foot.

The Pie Man's slacks, shoes, and neckerchief match his jacket, dingy white from head to toe. He mismatched the cloth buttons so that his collar is higher on one side than the other. To Baby the Pie Man looks like a homeless, dark-skinned Chef Boyardee. There's no trace of the freckles Baby got from his redheaded mama. The ones he catches hell for at school. The ones he tried to scrub off after reading the *Dred Scott* decision in American History the year before. But he know that even if his freckles won't come off, he could still hold it down for his people like Malcolm X, Tupac Shakur, or Lil Wayne.

Baby scratches the oval scab on his shin, thinking it's going to leave a mark when it heals. Maybe he'll cover it with a black fist tattoo when Mama's not looking. Touché wants everyone in the Mighty Black Ninja Krew to get black fist tattoos after they find and stomp Sanchez today. Baby's heard through the grapevine that Sanchez feels bad about what he did to Chaney, shot dead when the Mighty BNK—what Baby and his friends call themselves—tried to loot Sanchez's garage. It might be true that Sanchez felt guilt. Sanchez never held back telling Baby when he'd screwed up, but he was quick to give Baby props for good work, and he always gave Baby a can of cold drink at the end of the day.

Baby gets up to leave. But his mama yells at him and makes him sit his rear back in that chair right this instant. He's a target, she says, and Baby knows she's right. The Latinos have been dishing out hardcore payback. Curtis Thompson, the running back at Baby's school, got whacked in the knee with a galvanized steel pipe the other day. Curtis is out for the season, and with him any shot at the state championship. He said he never saw the guys that did it, but that they had Spanish accents. Nobody's safe, thinks Baby.

Baby's mama thinks she can help protect him by sending him to the barber. His hair makes him look like a maniac, she says. But Baby's afro is a matter of pride for him. It's a fuzzy crown that radiates out six inches going from black at the scalp to reddish brown at the tips. Like a halo made of rabbit's fur. Most of his friends think it's pretty cool. It counteracts the freckles.

One thing at a time, says the Pie Man to Baby's mama. Baby follows the Pie Man's lips. The way they form words. Inner tube round one second, then flat like the pair of rotten bananas in front of him. The Pie Man says he knows Baby doesn't want to go back on full house arrest. He looks at Baby as if expecting a response, which Baby doesn't give. Baby stares at those bananas. The Pie Man tells Baby to get up because it's time to get to work. Baby looks out the window. Orange traffic barrels flank a DO NOT ENTER sign at the end of the block.

"Nope," Baby says. "I ain't doing your slave work. If that means I'm stuck inside, then so what."

Baby's mama sprays air freshener at Baby. She tells him she'll turn him in herself if he doesn't get that haircut with the Pie Man. And he better be home before the streetlights come on. If he's more than a half inch from the front door by then, the SWAT team will come after him, she reminds him for the umpteenth and a half time. She kisses him on the forehead and leaves.

The Pie Man says he'll bring Baby to the barber now before they go to work, but doesn't get up from the couch.

He continues to stare at the empty space behind Baby. Baby rides his skateboard to the bathroom, where he straps on his Chuck Taylors and a pair of brown plaid shorts before climbing out the window.

• • •

The outside of Lawrence D. Crocker Elementary isn't much different from how Baby remembers. Lots of brick walls and stucco pillars. Plenty of rectangles. Gravel lot. The narrow plexiglass windows were faded opaque even before Baby and his friends went here, but the interior is totally different since Hurricane Katrina turned it out. Dried gunk coats the tile and baseboards. Green paint curdles from the floodwater pox. Rivulets of rust and mold syrup drool down the walls. Waterlogged books, tiny chairs coated in sludge, poster boards covered in blue-black fungus. The dump smells like anchovies pickled in urine.

Baby hasn't cut his hair but figures the worst that will happen is he'll get talked at more. He does skateboarding tricks on the retaining wall outside of the school, knowing it will be some time before the Pie Man puts his brain on and figures out where he is. But the van appears at the street corner within minutes. The clunker has one headlight and *Nobody Starves When the Pie Man's Around* scrawled in faded orange letters across the side. Ever since the Pie Man decided he's Baby's pops again, he's begun following Baby around in that death trap even when they're not working.

The Pie Man used to sell gumbo ya-ya, greens, and bread pudding at barbershops and car washes. Sometimes he makes pies—pecan, apple, and sweet potato—all with his own two hands. Baby can tell the Pie Man had been real proud of his business selling mouse balls to the citizenry. Baby chuckled when he remembered the web video he'd seen of a stupid toothless cat doing its best to gum a mouse to death. The mouse kept plopping out—pissed—but pretty much okay. Now, two-by-fours and tangled wires choke the van's bay. The Pie Man must have had breakfast, thinks Baby. He managed to button his jacket right and comb his flattop so that his head looks like an eraser, the way he likes. He must be sober.

"Why can't they just bulldoze this hole and start from scratch?" Baby says as he hauls a sledgehammer into the lobby outside of the cafeteria. Sanchez's tools were still at the jobsite. Baby thinks about how Sanchez's tools were for assembling things, not destroying them. Baby learned, to his own amazement, how to hang a door. It was harder than it looked, Sanchez told Baby, because you had to make many little decisions to get the right fit. Baby wonders what decisions Sanchez made before he shot Chaney. He lifts his sledgehammer and imagines swinging at Sanchez's head, watching his head soar into an outfield.

The Pie Man shrugs and tosses his jacket on a wheelbarrow. He has ink on his bicep. An eagle, perched above an earth and anchor, flaps its wings whenever the Pie Man flexes.

"You ever shot somebody?" Baby says.

The Pie Man slings a wide shovel onto his shoulder and says he shot two people.

"Did they die?"

The Pie Man shrugs and says, "They both died."

They work their way into the library, where red wall pennants form a frieze near the ceiling. Bookcases lean at odd angles, having dominoed during the flooding. All the books are on the floor, mush. As little boys, Baby and Chaney filed these books for the librarian as punishment after starting a food fight. The books now look like the food they threw, Cream of Wheat.

The Pie Man says he's not entirely sure about whether he killed the second dude. The second dude he shot was an insurgent with his finger on a trip wire. The whole convoy unloaded on him and any one of them might have gotten the kill shot, he says. Or, he tells Baby, maybe the hajji died of fear.

"What about the first one?" Baby asks.

The Pie Man shovels books into the wheelbarrow on

top of his jacket. He says the first guy was his friend Fred-die, the first person he met when he enlisted. He murdered Freddie dead. He tells Baby he's not sure if either situation matters because at war it's legit to kill, but if you kill one of your own you'd better have your reasons clean as a fresh latrine, which is what the Pie Man had. Freddie had flipped the fuck out and tried to mow down the boys in the mess with a fifty cal. The Pie Man capped him from behind with his M240, which took Freddie's arm clean off above the elbow.

The Pie Man says Baby and his boys shouldn't be so ready to go settle scores with that Spanish guy. Baby can go any way he wants, but that doesn't mean he has to. The Pie Man says Baby should just sit on his hands. Baby notices a corroded picture of Nat Turner clipped to one of the wall pennants.

"People will roll you, if you let them," says Baby as he points a finger from the Pie Man to himself. "I ain't trying to get rolled, you heard me?" Baby straightens to his full height. "We getting him tonight."

The Pie Man pops a pill and says he can't argue with that much. He says he can't argue with much of anything except that the VA could stop screwing around and send him better medication. The Pie Man's face is scrunched up again like he's confused. He says he ain't slept right since Kirkuk.

"Why you even join the Marines?" Baby asks.

The Pie Man says it seemed like a good way to go. They needed a chef, and he needed a job for the future he had mapped out. A fair exchange he thought at the time. But he never baked a single pie in the military. When he came home, he'd forgotten how to. Whether you get Sanchez or he gets you, the Pie Man tells Baby, you end up in the same place.

The Pie Man and Baby put on respirator masks. Baby thinks the Pie Man looks like a futuristic rat. Baby grabs the sledgehammer and zeros in on the face of Guy Bluford, the first brother launched into outer space. He swings and before long the walls are coming down all around him.

It's an hour to sundown, and the Pie Man left Baby once they finished work for the day. Touché and Turtle skate up the driveway in front of the school.

Touché does a 360 from a ramp angled over a mound of bricks and stops near Baby. "Welcome back to Genitalia." Touché's got a fauxhawk, and his striped hoodie makes it look like he's still spinning. General Taylor and Peniston are the streets closest to Crocker facing downtown. They've called the streets *Genitalia* and *Penis*ton since the sixth grade. *Dry-ass* Street runs perpendicular to them both, a few blocks closer to the streetcar line. "You still got your Oreo 'fro, little man?"

"Man, my mama can't make a brother cut off his trademark," says Baby, trying to ignore Touché's comment. Baby hates it when Touché makes fun of his size almost as much as he hates when he makes fun of the fact he's practically half White. It isn't Baby's fault his mama's pops wasn't Black like everyone else. Touché seems to know where everyone's buttons are. He's like a video game champ who's got all the codes memorized. *X* to kick you in the gizzards. *Z* plus *turbo* to take out your knees and dump you in Lake Pontchartrain. Sometimes you don't even know it was Touché who got you.

"Yeah, I asked your mama for a haircut. She gave me a blow job instead." Baby pokes his tongue against his cheek and pumps his fist. "The bitch still don't understand English."

"Your mama so fat," says Touché, "I pushed that ho in the Mississippi River and rode her to the other side."

"I heard in Sunday school," Baby says, "your mama so old she was Jesus's nanny."

"Your mama so fat she went to an all-you-can-eat buffet and ate the Chinese waitress," says Turtle. "She be using Ethiopians as toothpicks."

"Your mama—" says Touché, but he stops and punches Turtle in the shoulder. No one makes fun of Turtle's real mama. Not even Touché. Not since the last time they saw her, dry-skinned and strung out, begging for change on Canal Street. She wore a tank top and jeans so small they could have fit a ten-year-old, but loose enough to reveal her soiled lace underwear. "We need to get that Sanchez and pop him. *Whap.*" Touché clutches his board and brings it down on Sanchez's imaginary head. "Or drag him across town by a rope."

"Kill that noise," says Turtle, fixing his thick glasses on his nose. "We ain't getting nobody." Turtle grabs Baby's shoulder. "I saw the Pie Man's van earlier."

Baby always thinks he's staring at him from another world through those binoculars. A scarier world.

"He playing camp counselor again?" Turtle asks. Baby nods.

"Come on." Turtle skates off with his glasses in hand. He doesn't need them to get where they're going.

All three boys glide to the lot behind the school. Scraggly grass forms a crescent along the edges of the fractured concrete. It reminds Baby of the Pie Man's receding hairline. They enter a rusting cargo container where the Mighty Black Ninja Krew keeps gas canisters.

The Mighty BNK is what Baby and his boys do when they're bored. And for fame. Like the time they went berserk-boarding through the Catholic church by the house where Turtle's foster family lives. Baby videoed the others zipping across the checkerboard floors and leaping from the altar. Touché spray-painted "MBNK" on the wooden doors during their escape. On their way out, Baby noticed the statues of old men in the gallery above. They wore flowing pink sheets, one statue dangling a key, the other a sword. They looked like they wanted to kick his ass. He gave them the finger, as the Mighty BNK got away clean. Touché posted the video, which went viral on the web.

If he were being totally honest, Baby would admit he joined the Mighty BNK for the same reason as the others: to get laid. They hide their faces on camera with white stockings, but everybody at school knows who they are. It's worked out great for the rest of the Mighty BNK. It hasn't worked at all for Baby.

He doesn't have the swagger of Touché or the brains of Turtle or the wicked determination of Chaney. Baby's fourteen, but looks closer to nine since he's two heads shorter than the others and has no stubble on his chin and chest, and no pubes. When the girls at school call him Baby, they mean it.

Baby doesn't know the first, second, or third thing about girls, but takes notes and listens to the rest of the Mighty BNK talk about doin' it. Baby fears he'll die without doing it. He wonders if dying without doing it means he winds up in heaven as a kid for all eternity. Or in hell for a kid that wanted it.

Touché sniggers in the corner of the rusty cargo container, having gone first. His arms are tight against his chest. Baby knows this pose means to leave him be. Baby and the Mighty BNK jacked the nitrous oxide from Sanchez because they were tired of sniffing airplane glue and Freon, which burned the ever-loving b'jesus out of their noses.

Turtle fills a blue balloon from the nitrous oxide canister and hands it to Baby. Baby's careful not to let any gas escape. He glances at Touché, whose face is wet. He always cries when they fly.

Turtle tokes weed in a crouch. He offers to Baby, but Baby shakes his head. Baby takes a draw from the balloon, nearly as much as his lungs will hold. Then he sucks a bit of straight air on top to hold the gas steady. The nitrous is sweet on his tongue. Sweet and steady like he's just licked a birthday cake, like his birthday was yesterday, is today, and will be tomorrow. Seated and holding his breath, Baby clutches the tips of his Chuck Taylors. A tingling rips up his spine like electric spiders on parade. The spiders are angry this time.

They rummage through Baby's innards for flies, bad ideas, and mildew, but don't find enough to keep them alive.

Baby shoves the gas from his lungs. He feels like propeller blades are chopping him into finer and finer pieces. Every time he feels this, Baby wonders what it would be like to choose how he puts himself back together. Bigger and stronger this time. Taller and darker this time. This time hung like a mutant ox. Maybe this time feared by men and loved like a widow's diamond. Baby clutches his hair and falls onto his back, shivering.

They were good until the alarm in Sanchez's garage went off. Baby saw the flash of Sanchez's gun, and Chaney's eyes open as full moons on his way to the ground. After Touché and Turtle ran away, the police found Baby frozen in place, his sneakers covered in vomit, the only member of the Mighty BNK to ever be captured alive.

Touché finishes the weed before Baby gets a second tug at the balloon. Touché is tapping the side of the cargo container with the thick tree limb he sometimes uses as a walking stick.

"They running a terror campaign on all the Blacks in our 'hood." Touché flicks the spent bud away.

The gas has different effects on each member of the Mighty BNK. It makes Touché paranoid. Well, more paranoid than normal, Baby thinks.

"Them rednecks can't just shoot any brother they feel like," Touché says.

"That's dumb," Turtle says. "Sanchez ain't no kind of redneck." The gas brings out Turtle's argumentative side.

Sober, he would let Touché carry on until he got tired of hearing himself. "Old Sanchez's Hispanic."

"I don't care if he Jesus on the cross," says Touché. "His people coming over the borders taking our space, our girls."

Baby knows Sanchez didn't come over any border. Sanchez's son went to the same school as Baby's mama.

"And what about you?" Touché asks Baby.

Baby toys with his ankle bracelet. It's a hunk of plastic in the shape of a watch, a handless, faceless watch that refuses to let him know what time it is. Baby wonders what will happen after they get Sanchez. Maybe Sanchez didn't mean to kill Chaney, and it's not like a smackdown will bring him back. Baby raises his eyebrows as if to say, "What about me?"

"You so fake." Touché spits. "You need to man up."

"I ain't stomping some old dude," Turtle says.

"He shot our boy. He got Baby with a tracking band on his leg. But he gets to walk around scot-free. This is our neighborhood. Shit, this is our country." Touché started saying this after Chaney died. "We about to get a Black president. People can't screw with us like this anymore."

"Maybe we shouldn't have tried to take his stuff," Turtle says.

Baby skates past a one-way sign on Claiborne Avenue, his hair bouncing in the wind. A police car with its sirens going nearly sideswipes him. He salutes it, but trips to his knees in the process. That's what the gas does to Baby. It kills his balance. Baby looks around to make sure no one saw him and picks up his board. He hurries past an abandoned double the Latinos tagged with graffiti. He can't accept that his own neighborhood isn't safe anymore.

It's almost dark, and Baby's mama will start her checkup on him, calling from her night job scrubbing hospital sheets. She'll expect him to tell her he's safe and sound in their box of old people's feet.

Baby thought Touché and Turtle might fight over getting Sanchez. Touché kept pushing it, but Baby skated off. Touché called Baby a pussy.

Touché is in Baby's head as he skateboards home. Touché thinks Baby doesn't want to get payback for what happened to Chaney. But if Baby isn't willing to get Sanchez, what is he? Maybe Touché's right. A Latino man in overalls is perched on a ladder, applying stucco to the side of a two-story house. The lawn is littered with empty stucco bags. Baby hums a stone at the man, but misses. The man waves at Baby. Baby searches for another good rock, but the world disappears. His head is covered by a bag and he can't breathe. Something hard whacks him senseless, and even though he's defenseless, whoever's on top of him is having too much fun to let up. He kicks Baby in the stomach, and twice in the face. When Baby comes to, he pulls the bag off his head, but the attacker is gone. He wipes his mouth and finds blood and tooth fragments.

When Baby gets home, the Pie Man is asleep on the side steps, using a paint can for a pillow. Baby goes inside and looks in his mama's hand mirror. He's glad she's not around to see his nose is smashed or that he's missing half an eyetooth. Blood coats his chin, and the dust from the stucco bag makes him look like a ghost. He's afraid to wash the dust off, worried the water will activate the stucco mix and turn his head to stone.

Even his mama would agree somebody has to pay for this. If the Mighty BNK let this go on, pretty soon Baby, Touché, and every other kid in the neighborhood will be swinging from trees. Baby fingers the van keys from the snoring Pie Man's pocket. Every color in the rainbow is on the Pie Man's grungy jacket. Baby runs outside and hops into the Pie Man's van and cranks the ignition. The pedals are so far from the seat, making it hard to drive, but it's only a couple of blocks to Touché's.

"They rolled you like a blunt." Touché purses his lips in a mock whistle after he climbs into the passenger seat.

He almost seems to be enjoying this. Baby rubs his mouth, but the sharp pain stops him.

Although the bleeding has slowed, his jaw clicks when he moves it.

"Don't say I didn't try to warn you before," Touché says. "It's get or get got out here."

They stop at a gas station in Gert Town. There's a darkened church on the next lot. One of the neon cross arms is out, so it looks like a machine gun turned on its nose. Touché leaps out and disappears into the station. The lights are painfully bright to Baby.

Touché sprints from the gas station, toting a bottle. He hands it to Baby. It's a bottle of Goose.

"Should we go get Turtle?" Baby says.

"We don't need no pussies in the way. We mad dogs tonight."

Baby doesn't let the vodka bottle touch his sore lips when he drinks. Tilting his head back makes him woozy, but his insides swelter. He tastes ash and rust, and pours some onto the van floor.

"Why'd you do that for?" Touché says.

"That's for Sanchez," Baby says. "He's going to need it."

Touché chuckles and takes the bottle. "Yeah! That's what I'm talking about."

They drive to Sanchez's garage, and Touché and Baby slip white stockings over their heads. Baby's hair makes the stocking pooch out so that he looks like a lightbulb. It mashes the swollen parts of Baby's face, immediately making him want to take it off, and sandpapers the sweat-moistened stucco coating his skin.

It's still early enough that Sanchez is bent under a hood like he's praying to the engine.

Water tings as it circulates in the van radiator.

"Yo, old man Sanchez! What's up, *amigo*?" Touché calls out before they enter the wooden fence. Touché says "amigo" wrong. *Hi-meego*, he says.

"*Qué pasa, 'migo?*" says Sanchez, stuffing a rag into his overalls. He stops in place when Touché and Baby step into view. Baby figures Sanchez will take off running or go for a gun in his toolbox, but he doesn't. He rakes a hand through his thin, white hair. Baby thinks maybe the Pie Man will show up and slap Touché on the back and say they've had enough fun for one night. Instead, they stand in silence broken only by nature: crickets and toads rioting in the bushes.

Touché and Baby move forward, but Sanchez stands where he is. He's short. Not Baby short, but not much taller. "Move." Touché shoves Sanchez toward the van.

"You're Reverend Goodman's son?" Sanchez says to Touché. The stocking mask flattens out Touché's cheekbones and tweaks his nose downward, but he's still recognizable.

"You don't know me, *niño*," Touché says.

"Ian?" Sanchez says to Baby, calling him by the name Baby's mama only uses when she's about to lay down the law. "Why are you here?" Sanchez says just before Touché cracks Sanchez in the back of the head with the shaft of his stick. Sanchez falls, out cold. Baby smells copper, blood, and looks down at Sanchez's slumped body.

"It's on now." Touché laughs.

Baby thinks it's over, that they'll drive off and put this behind them, but Touché stoops and wraps twine around Sanchez's wrists and ankles. Touché tells Baby to help lift him to the floor of the van. Within minutes, they're speeding toward the levee on the back side of City Park. When they reach the muddy access road that shadows the levee, Touché nearly rolls the van. Sanchez clutches his knees on the bay floor. A dark landscape whizzes by as Baby grips the metal handles in the van bay. Baby's ankle bracelet vibrates.

He forgot it was there. He grabs the bracelet, but it keeps vibrating.

The van pitches when they scale the levee, causing a box of nails to fall on Sanchez. He yelps. Baby tries to catch the next box, but misses it. He feels like he's on a conveyer belt, heading toward an open furnace. Touché stops near the concrete floodwall, which sits atop the levee. He takes Sanchez's ankles, Baby grabs him by the armpits, and they haul him from the van. Sanchez is heavier than he looks. They drop him in the moist grass at the foot of the wall.

"Maybe we can just leave him," Baby says. His head is still fuzzy from what he drank and inhaled earlier, and from the beating. Touché remains silent and switches on his video camera. The van's headlight floods the scene so there's no color. Sanchez prays into his bound hands.

"You first." Touché hands his walking stick to Baby.

Baby steps toward Sanchez and water snakes in through the seams of his Chuck Taylors, sending a jolt up his spine. Sanchez looks up at him. The stick is covered with spikes. Touché added nails to it, Baby realizes.

"Take your shot, little man."

Crooked nails glisten like fingers in the moonlight. Baby brings the stick up high above Sanchez's head. Some of the nails are angled at the van. Other nails slant toward Touché, Sanchez, and the night sky. One points straight at Baby.

The Places I Couldn't Go

My good girl and me was happy as goldfish till she got pregnant. She would handle it. We agreed. She was in two-year college, and we was both busted. Who could pay for formula? Wipes? A car seat? I caught the bus to work.

But she switched up outside the clinic. I tried to talk reason, but she wasn't having it. Her cheeks were red as welts, but she wasn't crying.

"I thought you were better than this," I said. She left me outside the clinic.

I tried to get us back to the way things used to be. We always made out on her mama's couch. We did that one more time—I brought weed and nacho chips over—but the next time I stopped by her mama said she was gone and that I shouldn't come round no more.

I saw her years later. I worked a gas station register by an off-ramp. She still had those baby-fat cheeks. I bet she changed her hair a million times since last I touched her, but her hair was the same again as it was before.

She had a boy hanging round. He wore cleats and knee socks. There was a grass stain on his jersey.

I kept eyeing her, but she wouldn't look at me. She circled the racks and went to the automatic doors. They whooshed open, then closed, then open. She pulled that boy by the arm.

"Don't stare at that man," she said. "We don't know him."

Outside, a man pumped gas into their car, a convertible, and they all rode off together. I went to the window. They crossed the intersection and disappeared.

Spinning

One.

After my dad died, I bore his body from room to room.
The cancer had flayed his
      flesh.
I was shocked by his heaviness, his body
         pulled the cords of my back
                      to their conclusions.
      He put a violin in my hands when I was small, and
once I turned the peg as a note rose
                  higher and higher
     until the E snapped against my arm, a caterpillar-
shaped welt rising.

Two.

I refuse my father once:
       he asks me to gift him a pack of
       cigarettes.
       Grandmother has a heart attack alone in the night,
       arteries hardened by Philip Morris.
       A surgeon slices
       my mother's
                     breast
       to save her from cells gone to riot, chewing their way
                          out of her
                          body.
               I say, "Father, I'll do this for you but
               once." Love is.

Three.

Mama cries for years after his death. His leaving ends our
circling. "Don't you miss him, son?"
       The green wedge of a Salem's pack winks from
       her lap.
       After I filled my car's tank, the needle rises from E
       to F.
       Every cell of Mama's body balloon-filled with
       heavy water.

In my daydreams, she inhales—smoke nettles her
lungs—
then calls his true name.

Zero.

1982. I'm four. Dad takes the wheel of a pickup truck he
borrowed from work without permission, reaches over to
clip me into the passenger seat, throws the transmission
into drive, lights off down the ice black rock road of Veter-
ans Highway, watches my laughter at the witch's cackle of
wind flowing through the cabin, misses his turn at Lafre-
niere Park, turns too fast, spins us at the intersection, two
infants on the back of a mermaid, the fishtail whipping in
the drizzle-made ponds, he—reaching over to pin me in
place as I think

this will always be.

Fast Hands, Fast Feet

Nothing for me to get by on here. Bubble gum wrappers on the seat cushion. Can't use. Empty jugs strewn across the back seat. Can't use. Cassette tapes in the pocket on the door. Can't use. Who even still on cassettes, anyway? What year they think this is, 1980? A stash of brown nickels in the armrest. My stomach hum. I just might eat tonight, me.

I'm leant across the front seat of this hoopty. Windows fogged up from cold. A cat hiss on the hurricane fence in back of the house. This a quiet hood. A good place for checking car doors quick to see if they locked or alarmed. If they locked, move on. If they alarmed, move on triple time. If they ain't locked or alarmed, well, here I is.

I stuff change in my pocket, carve a middle finger in the dashboard, and lookie here. Someone left me a bedroll on the floor behind the seat. My arm shiver. Too much good luck a bad sign. It's time to run, but then I see a dude in a

camo jacket at the end of the driveway watching me, trap-
ping me. He big enough to knock down a tree with a
ah-choo.

"Ain't got to run from me none, girl." He put one hand
out like calm down, everything gonna aight, but his other
hand still at his hip. Just like a police do when he bout to
shoot.

Breath steam out my nose. Run for the street? He tag
me before I make the sidewalk. Crawl under the house?
Take forever and a day, plus I scrape up my knees something awful.

The cat hiss behind me. Yeah, you right, cat. Thank
you. You too kind.

"Take what you need," the dude say. "But just let me—"
He trying to have a conversation. But I been sent to Joe
Blackman Juvenile—the JBJ—once. Queen Elizabeth Two
asked me who am I to turn my nose up at a few months of
free housing? But I ain't trying to be in nobody's kennel just
for free grits. That's bird shit, that.

He still talking. He step forward. I step back and go.
That's it. Run for your life, girl. Hit the fence. Jump like a
jackrabbit with your tail afire. On the other side, I don't see
that cat nowhere.

· · ·

Best burger I ever have. I can borrow fruit from the froufrou
market before the tie-dye-shirt people see me. I can borrow
a bag of chips from the scuzzy corner store before the door

I come through swing close. Fast hands. Fast feet. Try and catch me. But I can't fry up a wad of meat and serve it nice on bread with crunchy onions and ketchup like this. Takes money, that. My first hot food since sunup a week back.

Make me think the man upstairs back on my team. But who knows? He probably sitting on the bleachers, shaking his head, checking his watch. Fifteen years of living, and we still ain't on good terms. Just glad to be home, me. Still, this ain't nothing like a proper house. The roof an overpass. Headlights peek through the gaps above. The walls is wet with oil and sparkly from cigarettes tossed out of windows. The floor was a cardboard flap, but now, in my tight corner, I have me this bedroll. I laid it out like a magic carpet fixing to take me to Zion.

They was some doodads tucked in the bedroll, a lighter, a metal cup, junk like that. There was a picture of a girl, that ain't junk. It hang on a chain. She got happy cheeks and I-love-you-forever eyes. I wonder what she wanted from whoever she was looking at.

Queen Elizabeth Two call this place her province. I guess she can call it whatever she want 'cause she been here since Jesus was a badass child, flipping tables at the mall. But Queen Elizabeth Two don't really live here. I don't really live here neither. The fifty-leven other people in tents and sleeping bags under this bridge, moaning and shouting in the cold, they don't really live here neither. It's a nobody home.

Someone grab my shoulder, but I duck out of it. I don't like fingers touching on me.

It's the dude from the driveway. How he find me? Ain't like I left my address. Looking up his legs like looking at two tree trunks. He could squash me like a cockroach and that would be that.

"I came to see you." The dude sit down.

"You crazy," I say. He say he not crazy. He Sergeant. Not Sarge, but Sergeant. He don't like when people call him Sarge. He didn't fight the Taliban for no abbreviations. "I borrowed some stuff from your car," I say and dump the comb, the lighter, and some other doohickeys between us, toward the bottom edge of the bedroll, near his feet. It's not a busy night in the province. Once I get to my feet, I can run in any which way I choose. "Was holding it for you."

"That wasn't my car," he say. "The owner out of town, far as I can tell. I been using it to keep from freezing my tailpipe off. How you put up with this frost, small as you are, I can't even figure." He shake his shoulders.

"Cold ain't never bother me." I wipe my nose with the back of my sleeve. My fingernails sorta blue. Maybe it is extra chilly tonight. He ask where my folks that look out for me are. I tell him I'm my own folks.

"I was trying to say to you before you ran off that it's all just stuff," he say. "You can have it. But the one thing I need back is that picture."

"Picture?" I ask. "I ain't take no picture." I take a lot of stuff, but I don't have anything I like. And, I like the picture. Really, I don't want to give the picture back. Still, something about the look on his face, more sad than mad.

I hand over the picture that was tucked under my thigh, and he squat down and lay it on the bedroll, all nice like. He flip open the lighter. A flame spring up in the dark like ta-da. Sergeant stare like there ain't nothing in the world except for that picture. Nobody ever look at me like that.

"You like her?" I ask.

"I'm guessing I do, but she dead and long gone." He lean closer to the picture, but he ain't smiling. I wonder why he don't just hold the picture in one hand and the lighter in the other, but his other hand still tucked into his pants pocket like back in that driveway. Lame arm.

Normal people trouble enough. Last thing I need is get caught up with a crazy, cripple-arm man. I hop up and walk away. Sergeant call after me. I could turn on the jets. I ain't think the big lump couldn't catch me. But before I know it, he right beside me.

"Where you going?" he ask.

"You got your stuff back." I go around a frozen puddle. A boot stuck in the middle of it. "Leave me alone, you damn fool." Sergeant frown like I just called his mama ugly, and I feel kind of bad for him, but the only person I even tolerate a little is Queen Elizabeth Two and that's just 'cause she can't actually talk.

Something crash nearby. Those two old drunks in top hats slap-fighting by one of the concrete pillars. They must have got into it again over a bottle of malt liquor and dropped it.

"You should go to a shelter," he say. "It ain't right out here." It ain't right in the shelters neither. People scoot up on you when they think you sleeping. Try to use your body like a pillow or worse.

Queen Elizabeth Two stumble our way. She dragging three or four blankets from her shoulders and carrying a lantern. Her tiara almost fall off, but she catch it. Then she do hand motions.

"What, she hungry or something?" Sergeant ask. But I know her signals. Hand to heart for badge. Fingers to eyes for look out. Thumb over shoulder for scram.

"She say it's time to get out the province. The man here." And, sure enough, a pack of vans parked on the corner. Men in blue wander into the province, long, black sticks in hand. They coming to protect and serve us. Somebody scream. Cars pull up on the street, blueberry lights flashing everywhere.

Sergeant put his hand on my shoulder.

"Man, I don't know you." I punch his hand away.

"You ever hear of going with the flow?" he ask.

"No," I say. We run straight.

We almost out of the province when a voice yells something about a freeze warning. Next thing I know, men in blue all around us. One of them grab my collar. They grab Sergeant, too. He muscles his way closer to me. His breath hot in my ear.

"Break for it when I say," he say.

"What?" I say, but he shove me away and rear up like a grizzly bear. I spin out from under the man holding me and run. Wind in my ears. Feet slapping concrete. Flying is the best feeling they is. I'm clear down the block. I stop by a dumpster and look back. The men got sticks in they hands, and they pounding Sergeant like bongos. He on his knees. They don't know he just a one-arm crazy man. They don't know he was only in the province 'cause I stole his ghost girl picture. It take four of them to get him cuffed and dump him in the back of a car. Sergeant bump the car door like he trying to get out, but he locked in. The men in blue go back to collecting people.

What I know? You never go back. When you run, you keep running till your lungs feel like a big bruise. You run till you fall on your face from tired. Then you get up and run till you all by yourself and men with fat fingers can't touch you or slobber on you or call you they pretty little thing. And I know God sitting on that bench, his arms folded, figuring that he know what I'm going to do. I'll say screw Sergeant, me. Sergeant got himself in this mess. Sergeant get himself out. But Sergeant the reason I ain't going back to the JBJ or whatever fucking hole they want me in.

I run back and check the door of the car he in. Wouldn't you know it! The damn thing ain't even locked from the outside. Sergeant make a goofy grin. Here I is, Sergeant. Let's fly.

There enough abandoned houses that we find one not very far away. It's an upstairs downstairs place, but we flop on the wood floor in the front room. Lights flash across the curtain. I open his lighter. He ask how I got his lighter back from him. Fast hands. Fast feet. It ain't nothing to take what

I want if I want it enough. Sergeant face look like old pizza, but he say don't worry, baby, he done took worse from better.

I sit with my back on the wall. He fumble in one of his jacket pockets and pull out wrapped-up, biscuit-looking things.

"Ever have Russian tea cake?" he ask.

"No."

"Well, you in for a treat." They look kinda dry, but I eat some. So tangy and sweet on my tongue. I done stole plenty of sweet treats, but they ain't never taste like this. "Thanks for helping me."

I shrug.

"I'm heading to Texas to find work," he say. "They say the money is good there about now."

"What you going to do with one arm?" Sergeant look down at his arm. My face get hot. I'm a dumb fool, me.

"You ought to come along." He lay on his back and put his good hand under his head. "I'll look out for you. When the last time you had a real roof over your head?" This ceiling leaking, a wet patch go from one end to the other. Other than the JBJ, I can't remember when I last slept inside. I ask him why he want to lug me around.

"Everybody need family," he say. "That picture was my daughter." I ask what happen to her, but he just stare at the ceiling.

A bit of tea cake left in the wrapper. I pinch that piece and put it in my mouth. It taste sweeter than its size. My mouth full of happy. I feel like I done lived in the province, where it's hard, cold, and smelly, my whole life. Is Queen Elizabeth Two family? Those two old drunks? The men in blue? The room green from the liquor billboard across the street.

"Imma go with you," I say. But Sergeant already sleep. He snore like he mean it. With his mouth open, teeth showing. I kick his lame arm. His belly go up and down. This ain't hardly what I want, crawling to Texas with this one. I can do bad by myself.

Sergeant jacket sprawled out to the side of him and that jacket got so many pockets full of goodies, I can hardly believe it. A pair of gloves. Too big, but warm. A flask full of water. I can use it. A roll of dollars. I find that girl picture and hang it round my neck. Time to run. Can't let my luck run out with this crazy, cripple-arm bum. I need a new spot where I ain't got to worry about nobody but me. Maybe I find something crosstown by the river. Watch the ships come in. I go to the door with Sergeant jacket rolled under my arm. The jacket huge like what they use to cover bodies in the province till the takeaway truck come. I don't need it for the cold, but it'll keep the rain off. Sergeant groan, lift his head, and clunk it on the floor. Damn fool. Can't he take care of himself for ten seconds? I bring the rolled-up jacket and stuff it under his head so he won't kill himself dreaming.

I stand over him, play with Sergeant lighter, watching that flame wink on and off. Then I curl up and use his dead arm for a pillow so I can sleep. I can fly tomorrow.

Election

I read the script verbatim, always starting with the line, "My name is Simone Winters and I'm calling because Roland Chereau cares about our town and you." I'd make twenty calls each hour, thirty if I had a lot of hang-ups. Roland wore crisp banker's suits with wingtips. One morning, he came to the campaign office with a vase of flowers, flowers not specifically for me, and yet flowers he placed right in front of me. As if the others wouldn't notice.

He made me one of his special assistants. I'd go with him to debates and fundraisers. Afterwards, I'd stand next to him trying not to make eye contact, my arms stiff against my sides. His tangy cologne in my nose. Each morning, I awaited his call. He'd rented an apartment on the outskirts and that's where he'd call for me to meet him at.

The last time I went to the apartment was the day after Roland won the election. We lay in bed. He was happy. So was I, of course. I knew better, but a part of me believed he would leave his wife and kids due to his newfound strength. He wouldn't care about the media questions. I was twenty-one years old and raindrops tapped against the window as if they were trying to get my attention.

The night before, during his victory speech, Roland's supporters hung on to his words for dear life. He spoke about how together they would solve all their problems once and for all. I asked him if he believed everything he said.

"No," he said. "But it makes folks feel better when I say those things. Part of the job description is to make people believe."

"Should I believe you love me?" I asked. Immediately, I regretted myself.

Roland was quiet for a few seconds, staring at shadows on the ceiling. He turned my way and I knew he was about to say something, so I put a finger over his lip.

The Sparer

I used to bully this kid. Braces. Always sick. Small and a whiner, too. Carlos's family lived in a shack lit by candles; they couldn't afford to keep the lights on. His mama was a maid and left early on weekends to get to the hotels downtown. Those were my favorite days because we'd play in the field next to his house. He'd watch us from his bedroom. Eventually, he'd come out so I could bust him in the mouth. Sometimes his sister, Lametra, gave me the eye, but I never took any trouble over it from their mama. I brought hell to that kid.

I came home from middle school one day and Carlos's house was empty with the lights on. I went up to the porch, and sure enough the inside was cleared out down to the cheap tile, which made sense. After all, his mama was a maid.

In college, I caught fights on the TV at the corner bar. I was watching intensely one night, when my buddy jabbed me.

"Look like you seen the girl of your dreams," he said, "the way you eyeballing that set, Eddie."

I told him that when I was younger I used to own Carlos, the wiry one in the red trunks. Everybody, my future wife included, was sure I would become a famous boxer before long. My buddy just laughed and poked my belly.

Years later, I was downtown with the family, just before I lost my good job. Carlos came strutting up the street, a full-grown man. I recognized him even in his expensive suit with a fine woman on his arm. I stopped him and asked if he remembered me. He gave me the once-over and said he sure did.

"We used to spar together," I told my kids. My wife looked at me with this real hopeful look on her face.

The boxer gave us each a nod and cracked his knuckles. I stepped back.

"That never happened," he said, and walked off with his girl.

Catch What You Can

Mama say you got to help her quit drinking for good this time. She promise five bucks for every bottle of booze you find around the place you live. You find a pint in an empty cracker box and another wrapped in plastic in the toilet tank. You find nine whole bottles. You going to be rich.

The bottle hunt is payback for what Mama owe you.

Yesterday, she raid your dresser drawer and take your grass-cutting money—a couple rolls of one-dollar bills—to the Time Saver and buy booze. Some people buy gum or cinnamon toothpicks every time they go. She get whiskey. She say she must have dropped the rest of your money coming out of the store. No telling with her. You don't care what happened. You just want your money.

"Put what you find on the counter in the kitchen." Mama sit at the vanity you pulled from the dumpster.

Papa always say people foolhardy to go casting off

valuable property. Papa himself found a silver money clip by the manager's office. He gave it to you.

Mama jab her cheek with a brush that look like a squirrel tail. "I didn't think there'd be a whole party's worth of alcohol."

"Thought there'd be a lot more," you say. The baby in the place downstairs crying. That little rat never shut up. You wonder how many little rats in the complex.

"Thought there'd be more? You a funny one." Mama stand and pinch your cheek. "At least my period over."

"Ugh." A nasty taste wash up the back of your throat. You'll never understand how Mama wasn't born with the part that keeps other people from saying shit like that.

"Oh, my baby, you must be hungry."

"Don't call me that. It don't sound right."

"You still my baby." Mama smile big.

You ain't trying to be her baby. The fridge empty. The pantry empty except for Mama's nasty-ass sardines. Your stomach empty, and Mama done got skinny. She looking like a plastic mannequin. You trying to be the richest fourth grader at Fannie C. Williams Elementary. You trying to eat.

"We'll get something to eat out." Mama smooth her wrinkly skirt.

"Out?" you say. "Where you going?"

"I'm going to get me a job," she say. "The only way I'm going to quit drinking that stuff is if I find something to do. You coming, too." She sling her purse on her shoulder.

"No, I ain't. I got money to make, yards to cut." Papa always say summertime in New Orleans is a grass cutter's dream. It be hot as a skillet, but the grass don't burn on account of how much it rain. You can stuff your pockets cutting lawns that never stop growing dollars.

"I need you with me."

"You can't work," you say. "You'll lose that government money you just got."

"So? I went most of my life without it. I can do that again."

"It ain't bright to give up free money."

"Welfare making me sick," she say. But you thinking being broke making both of you sick.

Mama swerve the station wagon onto the highway ramp. Your mower rattle in back. You want to bring it in the apartment for safekeeping because people be stealing anything that ain't hidden from sight, but Mama say it's too rusty. It's Papa mower, but he let you use it. Mama say you too young to be cutting grass, but do you think she know what you too young for? No.

"Say you proud of me," Mama say.

"You proud of me," you say.

Mama cover her mouth and laugh that chirpy laugh she got. Makes you laugh, too, even though you wasn't trying to. This ain't the first time she talk about cleaning up, ain't the first mention of a paying gig. Last time, she lasted a week at the gas station before they fired her for drinking up the beer.

"You going to get a job that pays a lot?" You chew your

grape taffy, and like how it sticks to the roof of your mouth. You give Mama one. She like it, too.

"It ain't so much about the money." Mama squint in the rearview mirror. "If you always fretting about money, that make you ugly inside."

Your heart beat in your cheek. What Mama know about anything anyway? It ain't like you trying to buy Adidas tennis shoes. You doing what Papa say do. You making money like you supposed to. Doing what men do.

"Where we going?" you say.

"In town," she say. "I'll get me a job working at that sundry shop, the one by the Superdome. They sell your candy, too."

"The news people say things closing up in town."

"A little faith, son."

Poydras Street run down the middle of town. Mama and you ride in the shadow of the skyscrapers. Mama park by a brown-and-black building that look like a tall man in a suit.

"We can't park here," you say.

"Say who?"

You point at the NO STOPPING sign.

"Aw, boy, they ain't going to mess with this car none."

Mama and you walk to the sundry shop a couple of blocks from where the car is parked. A bunch of cardboard boxes heaped on the sidewalk. Orange CLOSING signs all over the windows.

You go in your pocket for more taffy, but you out. You start to tell Mama you told her so about the store, but you don't like how she look. Most of the time, she look like she fixing to burst out laughing, even when nothing funny going on—even when she mad—but that look gone now.

"I guess we too late for this one," she say. She turn around and watch you digging in one of the cardboard boxes. They full of brand-new mugs that say *World's Fair*. "Quit that."

You look up at her.

"Boy, don't you cut your eyes at me," Mama say. "We don't go through nobody trash."

"But this is all free stuff." You get a mug and rub it like a genie lamp. "We could sell these to people and make some money."

"Put that down." Mama clench your wrist. The mug crack on the curb. "We ain't that hard up."

You shake her off and say "Lookit." There's a place across the street that got windows like mirrors. Mama and you look little in the reflection. You been there before—they give out jobs—but they didn't help Mama out none. She bite her lip. You know we have to try them again, that that's the only real option.

The waiting room full of white folk, everybody in suit-and-tie, pantsuits and dresses. Mama glance down at her jean vest and pull the edges together to cover up her glittery blouse.

"Did you bring a book for you to read?" she ask.

"No," you say. You used to read all the time. Mama call you her "college boy" or "little professor" because you read Ms. Zora Neale Hurston and Mr. Ernest Gaines, but you stop because she don't deserve to congratulate you, the way she mess everything up.

She fill out paper on a clipboard and leave it on the counter. When Mama turn away, the lady behind the counter wrinkle her face like she got palsy. After we wait a while, the lady in the back, who keeps tracks of the jobs and who keeps calling Mama "babe," say she didn't think Mama would be back so soon, babe, and that all the positions are filled for the day, babe.

"There must be something out there," Mama say.

"Nope," the lady say, "we don't have nothing. Why don't you come back in a month or so, babe?"

"You think y'all have more jobs in a month?" Mama ask.

"I don't think nothing."

Mama thank the lady and take you by the hand. You know something ain't right because Mama never pull you around by the hand since you ain't a baby no more. She stop at the door and stare back at the lady like she want to say something, but she don't.

Mama and you try a few other spots. You go into a jewelry shop with cases of sparkly rings and watches, but they don't need nobody. By noontime, your stomach growl so loud you can both hear it. Mama look like she fall over if you push her with your pinky finger.

You wish Mama and you could go to Auntie Rosamond's, Mama's great-aunt, for some red beans. She always had good beans and rice, but now she dead. Mama get sad whenever you bring Auntie Rosamond up, so you don't anymore. She was into hoodoo and used to say something bad was coming. Guess she was right.

"How about we go to McDonald's?" you say.

"That stuff ain't hardly no good."

"We got to eat something."

"I know, son."

You back on Poydras, walking toward the river. A big ship, big as a skyscraper knocked flat, float by, hauling metal crates. Papa say those crates got anything you can think of inside: bikes, footballs, Atari games. You wonder if the crates got anything you want.

"I thought we parked about right here?" Mama ask.

"We did." You nod up the street. A white tow truck pulling the station wagon away. It look like an old man with a sack of potatoes on his shoulder. Mama and you lock eyes, and the way she look make your stomach drop. You know she can't afford to get it out from the pound, you know the car is long gone, and probably the cash money she offered earlier, too. You know that the ride downtown was the last ride in that car and you know you don't get to say bye to it.

"Don't worry about it," you say. "Sometimes these things happen for a reason."

"You starting to sound like me," she say. "It's not the car I'm worried about, though." She shake her head.

"My mower!" you suddenly realize. You run up the street, but that tow truck don't slow none. You turn and look at Mama. She standing with one hand on her chest.

"How we going to get it back?" you say.

"I wish I knew," she say, walking over to you. Mama try

to put her arm around your shoulder, but you spin away before she wrap you tight.

"How I'm going to cut people grass?" you ask.

"We'll get it back."

"How?"

"I'll work it out."

"No, you won't," you say, moving out of her embrace. You kick over a garbage can and a red mess spill out. Up and down the street, garbage cans everywhere. And you thinking they all filled with red messes.

"You never work anything out," you say. You cover your face with your fists.

"It's alright."

"No, it ain't," you yell. "Nothing's ever alright. We broke, and now I can't even make money."

"That ain't hardly for you to worry about, son."

"One of us got to. You ran off the man who used to handle that kind of worrying."

Mama pull back like she surprised. You think most other mamas would slap you a good one for being too frisky, but your mama never been that type of mama. She root around in her purse, but don't take anything out. She walk toward the French Quarter like she on a hunt. You follow.

Nobody inside Patty Chan's Great Wall Restaurant but the people that work there. You don't care because your stomach sounding like a bad dog. A paper dragon droop from the ceiling. A big water tank right inside the front door. The tank full of big, dark crawfish. They scramble over each other like they playing tackle football. All you smell is salt.

"How much money you have?" Mama say. You feel bad about what you said to her, so you give her your money clip with no back talk. She check her purse and say you can split yaka mein and a couple egg rolls.

A Chinese man curse at the water tank. The tank leaking. Water dribbling into a plastic bucket. No food on the buffet, just empty metal pans.

"I guess we can sit anywhere we want," Mama say. An old lady roll silverware into a cloth napkin. Mama pick a table by her. The menus already on the table, trapped under glass.

"We should get one." Mama nod at the tank.

"Those big crawfish-looking things. You kidding?"

"Those are lobsters," she say, "and I'm so hungry I could eat anything bout now, but I don't want anything. I want me something nice."

"Well, I don't want nobody's sea monster."

"I bet you'll like it. They a delicacy, cost a lot."

"You had one?" She shake her head. You wish she would lie. You wish she would say that she had lobster one time, and it changed her life like a hoodoo spell.

The old lady slide from her seat with a dip like she about to dance. Her red shirt ain't got no collar. Her hair curl like smoke.

"We'd like some yaka mein," Mama say.

"No, ma'am," the old lady say. "No yaka mein."

"Egg rolls?"

The old lady frown, and then she smile. "We have a limited menu. This is our last day."

"It seems like such a nice place to be closing," Mama say.

"It was." The old lady look around. All you see is cracked paint and these dusty fake flowers on the table that make you want to *ah-choo*.

"I tell myself thirty-five years, time for something else," the old lady say. "Me and my husband are going to Alaska. I've never seen snow."

The man from the tank walk over and wipe his glasses on his T-shirt. "Did they order?" the man say.

"We was trying," you say, "but you ain't got no food."

"Don't be rude, Gene," Mama say.

"I like you," the woman say to me.

"I like me, too," you say.

"Pick what you want," the woman say, "and I'll give it to you free. I'm Patty. He's John."

You grinning like crazy. Mama wink at you. Papa always say you never ever turn down free stuff because most of the time life give you less than you have coming to you. Catch what you can.

"I want me a lobster," you say.

John glance back at the water tank. The lobsters just sitting there like they on break.

"Pick one," John say.

You go to the tank, all four of you. Mama put her hand on the glass. One of the lobsters jump at her. She yell and jump back.

"You better do it," she say.

Most of the lobsters hanging out in one corner, but one is all by himself on the side that's leaking. He bigger than the others. Maybe they're a family and he's the man-of-the-house lobster.

"That one," you say.

"Not that one," John say. "He no good."

"What's wrong with him?" Mama say.

"He look okay to me," you say.

"John is right." Patty lean forward and tap the glass. "He injured his thorax."

The lobster creep backward. It got a hole in its neck.

"Claw fight," John say, "but the band on his claw came loose, so he won." You say you want that one.

John scoop the lobster out with his bare hand. Patty and John go into the back and a few minutes later, the lobster come out on a long platter with a cup full of melted butter and some noodles. The lobster is split right down the center so you can see all the pink-white meat. You wonder if this what a brain look like.

But Mama don't move, she looking off staring at nothing. You know she sad, probably thinking about what you said about Papa. Maybe she missing him. She ain't eating so you don't eat, until, after a while she say, "You not going to try any of that lobster?" she say. "They cooked it special for you and everything."

"I changed my mind," you say. "I don't want none."

"Why?"

"I shouldn't a said you made Papa go away."

Mama take your hand. "It ain't your fault he gone, and it ain't mine neither. We going to move on. Just you and me and not think about him."

"He ain't coming back?"

"I don't know, but that ain't for us to worry about, you hear? That's on him." Mama reach in her purse, pull out her flask but don't drink. You missed one. The old lady in the corner looking at Mama.

"But we family," you say. "Family can't forget family."

"Sometimes you got to roll with what you got," Mama say. "Things will get better. You watch."

You guess her having a flask mean the deal is off, that you won't be getting your five bucks a bottle. Are you looking surprised? No. You seeing what you thought you would see.

"I don't think so," you say. You poke the lobster, and it stare back at you. You bet it taste like one of Mama's nasty-ass, sour sardines.

Mama cut a piece of lobster tail. She dip it in butter and pull it up to her mouth. But she don't bite. She slide her plate over to you. Then she get up with her purse full of booze.

"Where you going?" you ask.

Bathroom, she say. She tell you to wait. Just wait for her.

Steam float off that lobster back. You grab Mama fork. You bring the bite up to your nose. It ain't like what you thought. It smell like honey.

Zimmermann

Some of the old houses too far gone. You only get by in this hustle by knowing when to work it and when to tear it down to studs. Got to have a good crew, too. That Zimmermann showed up one wet morning to the double I was working. I ain't trust him. He was a scruffy little cat and smelled of whiskey. I left to check another job. But when I came back, he had trimmed out the whole living room. The crown molding so clean, it looked like a dollhouse.

Still, Zimmermann came on the job wasted sometimes, and I made him sleep it off in his rusty pickup. On paydays, he went right to the closest liquor store as soon as I cashed him out.

One day, he showed up straight, his hair combed and his eyes clear.

"My girl's back," he said.

There was always a girl.

We was tightening up a ranch house in Lakeview when

she rolled up in a hatchback. That chick, Stace—she was okay for a skinny, white girl. Still, I ain't like having her around. A girl on a job bad news. Anyway, I can't fault nobody for their love relations. She had Zimmermann's heart in a box. I never saw him drunk again.

Stace pulled up one morning in Zimmermann's pickup. The doc told her that he'd seen it a thousand times: a drinker goes clean and his body can't modulate without the stuff. The dry rot finally catch up. I asked Stace why she'd come to town for that Zimmermann anyway.

Stace flipped her hair back and stared at the house behind me.

"I couldn't stand the thought of him killing himself slowly."

Glamour Work

When I was on juvie probation, the judge made me work with a caterer named Johnson. Johnson wore a yellow flower in his suit pocket. I ain't like peeling potatoes and hauling boxes of tomato sauce. But, real talk, it beat being locked up.

Johnson was busy. We got sent to all kinds of functions. I did the same thing at all of them: washed out empty bowls, took out the garbage. Glamour work.

The biggest event of the year was for the mayor during Mardi Gras. All the politicians and money people would be there. I usually worked in back, but that night Johnson hooked me up with a tux.

"I want you to go out there, Gene," he said with a smirk. "Learn something."

I'd never seen anything like Gallier Hall. A thousand people in their best. The men as sharp as broken glass; the women wore dresses that tossed light all over the room.

I was refilling a punch bowl when a white security man grabbed my shoulder and brought me to an office with a bunch of little TVs. They said I'd stolen some lady's purse. The video showed me close to the scene, but not actually taking nothing. When he didn't find anything on me in the kitchen, they let me go. Johnson said he had to fire me; he caught too much flak for having troublemakers around. He looked sad. I think he wanted to keep me.

The next morning, I went to chill with my boys. Ain't none of them around no more. They asked me if I was still working with that cook and I told them nah. I made up a story about how he'd fired me for joyriding in his delivery van, and they had a good laugh.

I wish I could have told my boys the truth about everything I'd seen at that gala, all those people just *living*, but I knew they wouldn't get it.

Before I Let Go

The paper's edge slits Gailya's thumb. It was six months ago when the first of the white envelopes appeared. In time, they showed up more often, multiplying as if carried by the magic owls in her daughter's favorite childhood book. Now, they flutter through the door's rusty mail slot every day, just after dark, landing like paper airplanes full of flat, angry passengers.

Each envelope hides the same correspondence: a folded sheet of ruled yellow paper printed with text made to look like handwriting. The message is always a variation of *I'm new to the neighborhood. Your house is great. I will buy it, I will pay your burden, and you won't be sorry.* Followed by a phone number. Followed by a printed signature made to look like handwriting. Followed by a laughing emoji. The address says the sender is only a few blocks away, but Gailya knows no one lives there. Short-term renters use the house, visitors like the tourist couple thumping the headboard on the other side of her double shotgun house at this very moment. Their rental SUV squats catty-corner by the lot where John Jackets lived until last year when his ten-year home repair ended with him sliding off the roof to the pavement, twenty feet below. Gailya watched it happen, saw the aftermath. The way he lay crumpled on the pavement like a puppet after the puppeteer goes to smoke a cigarette. John Jackets eyes bugged from the impact. Strings of blood strewn across the concrete. The letters are probably sent by a white man in Connecticut. Or a computer in Connecticut. Gailya sucks the iron flavor of her thumb.

Someone bangs on her door. When she answers, a lanky white girl with a nose ring—one of her renters—tries to step right into her house. But a firm hand to the shoulder stops the girl from entering. The girl's cheeks are flushed, her tattooed shoulder sunburned.

"Your door is on the other side," Gailya says. Music plays just like every morning. Her rude neighbor in the house behind hers is playing Frankie Beverly and Maze on his trumpet. The notes echo off the fronts of the houses across the street.

"We were wondering if you could clean our place," the girl says. "Like maybe change the sheets and the throw rug in the den. We've had a day."

"This ain't a hotel, and I ain't the maid. You paid for a place to lay your heads. You didn't pay for me." Gailya pushes past the girl, locks the iron security door, and descends the steps to her hatchback.

"But we could," the girl yells after Gailya.

"If you funk up my house, I'm keeping your deposit."

Gailya picks up two fares on the way to work but rejects a third when it appears on her phone. Her main gig for the night starts in ten minutes. She can't risk driving way out to Lakeview even if it would help her meet her daily savings goal, money she needs to pile up to keep her house off the city's tax auction block. Three houses in her neighborhood were sold out from under their owners just last month. She's making okay money but is many thousands of dollars short. No matter. She can't miss the gig. As it is, she barely had time to get into her waiter's shirt, waiter's slacks, and waiter's clip-on bow tie. An outfit that reminds her of the tap-dance lessons her mama brought her to when she was a child. The recital was in an upscale mall downtown beneath the wreaths and garlands of the holiday season. During her class's set, a couple of shoppers watched Gailya on the raised platform. At one point, one of the brown-haired women pointed at her as if to say, *Yes, that's the one I want.*

She slips into the kitchen at the back of the Garden District mansion just in time to hear Jake's speech, and just in time to see Coleen smirk at her as if to say, *Perfect timing, hot stuff.*

"That's the job," Jake says. The grapevine says he's an ex-con for kiting checks and other two-faced crimes. He can't even return to where he came from in Oklahoma because of an arrest warrant. But he's related to the owner of the catering company. Gailya never met the owner despite having worked for the company off and on for over five years, in addition to driving other people around, watching other people's chirren, and staring at other people from in front of the stage at concerts. That last style of gig always makes her chuckle. Security guard. As if she could stop even one of the onlookers with their expensive cellphones and cheap sunglasses should they get it in their heads to rush the stage, climb it, and take over.

"I want a good flow." Jake gestures at the marble counter next to the sink. "Irregardless of how packed it gets in there. Alternate hot apps and cold apps." He uses the word *irregardless* too much. "After the first forty-five—irregardless of how much savory stock we have left—we'll break out the mini tortes and pies. I tried them. They're tasty. Irregardless, don't you eat any." Jake looks directly at Gailya. A couple of the others laugh as the group disbands.

Coleen pinches Gailya's side. "Hey there, baby girl." She clucks her tongue. "What's your wedgie?" Gailya doesn't like when Coleen calls her baby girl. Partly because Coleen is as tall and skinny as one of the Canal Street palm trees the city strings with lights each fall. The height difference sometimes makes Gailya feel like a child in a way that makes her feel less than. Gailya is a grown-ass woman. A mother of a grown-ass daughter. A grown-ass homeowner. Still, she lets Coleen calls her baby girl. It's annoying but it makes her smile, which are the two best reasons to know anyone at all. They used to go together but Coleen is a better friend than lover. She likes to own things too much.

Coleen chars broccoli with a torch. She did carpentry work before a doctor told her to get out of the sun. But she's good with food, too. Building houses and building food are in the same family.

"Watch out for Jake tonight." Coleen sprinkles sea salt. "He got dumped."

"I ain't studying about that fool," Gailya says. "Let's get on with these broccoli things."

"Tell me your secret. You got another note from your admirer?" Both women place a broccoli thing in their mouth. Coleen chews and talks with her mouth open. "You're just mad because this secret man is more into your house than he's into you."

Gailya is annoyed by that kind of talk since Coleen ain't got to worry about her accommodations. Her house is paid in full. And for another thing, she's white. Like the people moving in and buying up everything in Treme. The black and white issue isn't just a black and white issue. It's a money and power issue, too, but it's no accident that people with money and power tend to look like Coleen. It comes down to who is willing to take without asking. Coleen grew up and lives just outside the city in St. Bernard Parish, where they used to burn down schools that let in Black folk. Those schools burned because the Black folk couldn't stop them. And Gailya and her neighbors losing their homes because they can't stop them. Stealing education and stealing housing are also in the same family.

The catering event might be a fundraiser for a hospital, literacy program, or arts organization. Gailya doesn't half concern herself with the causes because she's too busy thinking of her own causes, all the issues she has that twist her stomach into knots. She looks at the patrons and thinks, *You paid a grip to eat burnt broccoli. Give me your money. I'll get you some real food.*

Twenty minutes into the night, Gailya trips on an extension cord by the upright piano. She falls on one knee, and her food tray tumbles. No one notices her in the corner where it happens. Or they all pretend not to notice her. She only loses a single morsel in the fall, a mushroom. Sure that everyone is still pretending not to see her, she wipes the mushroom on her pants leg and tosses it into her mouth.

All evening, Gailya feels like her phone is ringing. She doesn't know if it's actually ringing because the device is in the utility room where the workers are made to place their personal belongings, but her daughter, Lea, always calls around this time. Midway through her shift she gets her phone, which had been ringing. Lea lives in Tokyo, where she teaches English to the chirren of wealthy businessmen and occasionally dresses up like what seems to Gailya to be a robot crawfish. What did she call it? Kobe? Copay? Coldplay? It's bedtime on Gailya's side of the planet, but the opposite for her daughter. Lea is always waking up into a better world.

"You should just sell it, Mama," Lea says on the line. "Go to Atlanta. You never liked our house anyway. Always calling the plumber for those tired pipes. Too many second line parades making noise, as much as you hate noise, and you can't afford those taxes on what you make anyway, now can you?" She's right. It had been a struggle enough to

cover the mortgage before a website declared her neighborhood the hottest neighborhood in the country thanks to the
white folk who were buying in and opening coffee shops
with silver chairs. Her property is worth more than ever
these days. All she has to do is sell out. And if she can't pay
up, she'll lose it anyway. But it had been her mother's house
and her grandmother's before. Black woman owned and
Black woman operated for three generations. Her mama
had almost paid off the mortgage by the time Gailya inher-
ited the house. Shame on her for getting a second mortgage
for repairs after the storm ripped the roof off and let in the
rainwaters. Ruined everything that wasn't made of porce-
lain or stainless steel, which meant she and Lea had a sink
and toilet, but no clothes, photos, or floor to stand on. It
was John Jackets who got her house straight when he was
younger and stronger. If he wouldn't have fixed her house,
he would have been younger and stronger when he went to
fix his own, and he might not have slipped like he did.

The city wanted its money in a couple weeks. If she was
in a movie, her neighbors would hold a fundraiser for her at
the last second. Someone would knock on her door. The
parish sheriff would be standing there with a gang of deputies, guns on their hips, court papers in their hands. But
voices would yell from down the block. They would be
walking down the sidewalk toward her porch: Retired Principal Holmes, Good-Time Martin, Mr. Dexter, who used to
run the corner store, and more would be marching toward
her with an oversized check to match their oversized smiles.
We got you, they'd say.

But most of her old neighbors are gone. They couldn't afford to rebuild like she had, so now they called other places home. Places like Houston, Atlanta, or Providence Memorial cemetery out in Jefferson Parish. Her new neighbors love her house, not her. She heard somewhere that every time a white family replaces a Black family, the block's home values jump up about 5 percent. Gailya wonders if there's a place in the world where she can be a duck instead of a goose.

"Why you always think Atlanta the answer to everything?" she says into her phone. She pops a mini cherry tart into her mouth. It's warm and sweet on her tongue.

"Ms. Trudy seems to like it a lot, Mama," Lea says. "Her beauty shop is doing great." Trudy and Gailya worked together in a raggedy shop for years. No heat in the winter and termite swarms each May. They were popular; Gailya never did less than ten heads a day. That was how Gailya paid for Lea's private school. But between Trudy's son being shot by the police after a parade and her Gentilly house going under water in the storm, Trudy left and never looked back. Gailya had seen the photos on Facebook. Trudy's Atlanta salon looked like something out of a magazine at the doctor's office. All kinds of celebrities claimed her now. Singers. Rappers. Even Oprah's friend passed through once. Trudy, who lost her keys every day and twice on Saturdays.

"I ain't moving to Atlanta, Lea. Everybody there think they too much."

"What do you want, Mama?"

"How about a little peace?" Gailya can't remember having ever been asked what she wants. She flips through things she might very well want—start a daycare center for special needs chirren, drink cocktails on a tropical beach, be involved in a protest march with hundreds of other women—but she realizes those are other people's dreams. Pictures she saw on her phone.

"Gotta go, Mama. My class starts soon. You know how Mr. Odagiri gets if I show up late."

When Gailya slips her phone back into her purse, Jake is standing by the door shaking his head.

"I thought I told you no more calls on shift," he says.

"You did."

"And not to eat food while on duty."

"Well."

"I'm going to have to let you go."

Gailya isn't about to get fired by some fugitive criminal supervisor. She has as much a right to her job as he does to his. But she doesn't even have the owner's number anymore. Lost it with her last phone.

"I need this job," she says. "I got to make these payments to the city."

"You should have thought of that before you ignored the rules again, miss."

"Miss? You don't even know what my name is, do you?"

"Irregardless."

Later, with Coleen in the passenger seat, Gailya takes a couple of food pickups from the phone app. The first is an Irish bar and grill. The second is a restaurant in an old firehouse with symbols, half-filled circles, and backwards letters instead of a name. The package from that one smells flowery, as if the food should be dumped into a vase instead of eaten.

At both drop-off houses, Coleen runs with the food to the tops of the steps. Gailya switches off the radio, relieved when the swirly jazz music fades away.

"I can't make my payments without that job," Gailya says when Coleen scoots into the car, after running up the steps of the second stop. "It was my best steady income."

"What if the guy who wants to buy your house is a Good Samaritan?"

"What?"

"Like he wants to buy it so that he can give it right back to you." Coleen pinches Gailya's arm, and it stings. Gailya frowns. "Sorry."

"You ain't helping."

"Look," Coleen says. "I'm staying positive because I know you'll work it out."

"You really think?"

"You belong here," Coleen says.

Gailya puts her hand on Coleen's.

"Someone should tell them people that." Gailya flips open the job app on her phone that lists tasks people need done. It seems there are all kinds of ways to make money, but nothing that will make her big money. She feels like a snail crossing a frying pan.

*　*　*

The next morning, Gailya is out of the house around dawn for the early service at New Spirit Baptist Church. It's the same old orange brick building from her childhood with white doors that lead onto orange carpet. The foyer smells of flowers from whoever had a homegoing there last night. The visitation book still sat next to the double doors.

Gailya always sits in the back to avoid making too much eye contact with people who don't like her type. People who shake their head at her for liking women. Lea once asked her why she went to a place where she felt like an outsider. But she didn't feel like an outsider. Everybody wasn't like that. Decades of coming to New Spirit almost every week haven't convinced her that the people there have the keys to heaven, that heaven is what they say it is, or that by showing up and putting bills in the silver tray means Jesus will give her a car, give her a mansion, or give her a private jet. But she believes that something made her and that something, whatever it might be, is good. She doesn't know how else to show her gratitude than to visit this branch of the Lord's Kingdom. Like making a deposit at a bank.

But more than anything, she loves to see the people who still live in her neighborhood. Deacon Bronson, who is in his eighties, still sits in the front pew in his bright blue suit. During the sermon, he says *yeah* every time Pastor Smith needs some hype. Janice Clark is three rows from the front in one of her handmade silk hats. A girl, the young niece of a high school classmate, who always rocks her baby girl on her shoulder. The baby was crying before, but now she stares at Gailya with the biggest browns.

After the service, Gailya climbs down the back steps in flats—she doesn't do heels, it doesn't make sense to walk around off-balance. The sun is bright, and just as she raises a hand to her forehead to block the glare someone taps her shoulder.

"Hey, auntie," says DeShawn. His wife and kids, a boy and girl under ten, are with him. Gailya is not really his aunt. But everybody in Treme calls everybody else *cousin* or *auntie* or something like that. DeShawn was a teen when he would show up and sweep out the salon. Gailya used to give him a twenty— more than the job was worth—every time. DeShawn went to community college and got himself an electrician's certificate.

"You doing alright, Ms. Gailya?" his wife, Paris, says.

"I'm making out okay, baby." Gailya steps in line behind the kids for supper, and leans forward to be heard over the others. Styro containers of food are a few more dollars than they used to be. When she was a girl, they were a couple dollars, but a few more dollars ain't bad. "These pork chop plates look good."

"Sure 'nuff," DeShawn says. "I don't mess with pork now, though. Trying to eat better. Heard you asking around about work. My connect at the casino hotel say they got spots in housekeeping. They paying right for anyone pass the felony check. Misdemeanors are okay, though."

"That right?" She and DeShawn both laugh.

Gailya didn't remember asking anyone about a job. She would have been too ashamed. But maybe they could tell just by looking at her. By the way she walked or talked. That's how family was. She stood up straighter. Still, in all her years of getting by, she's stayed clear of the hotels. Her mother had told her she was too good for that work.

One day, when Gailya was about eight, her mama came in the house, with the blue vinyl bag she kept her lunch in, muttering as she sometimes did, rainwater running down her stockings and into her shoes. She took the narrow stairs up to the converted attic that was her bedroom. As always, Gailya bounced up the steps after her with the newspaper because her mama loved the funnies. Gailya loved to sit next to her while her mama pointed out the shenanigans of cats, dogs, and people with problems small enough to laugh at.

Mama dropped onto her bed, and Gailya helped remove her shoes. The water made suction so that each one came off with a pop.

Mama patted her own face with a towel Gailya gave her. Her mama's face young, even though she was gray haired.

"What you want to be when you grow up, my little baby?" her mama asked. *My little baby* because Gaily was stick-figure skinny into her late teens.

Gailya normally blurted out what she wanted, but she had been watching some police detectives on a TV show the other day, and when she told Ronny Jones that she wanted to be a cop at recess, he said that was dumb, but she could be the lady who answer the phone.

Gailya twisted her foot under her.

"Well, I'll tell you one thing. Make sure you do what you want to do. Do something that fills you up."

* * *

That afternoon, Gailya completes an application and hands it to the white woman with the rose-tinted glasses. The woman flips through the pages, licking her thumb for ease of flip. She stops flipping and looks up. Gailya hopes she doesn't decide to call Jake at the catering company for a reference. She was only fired last night, but that job already feels far in her past, like a streetcar sliding in the opposite direction.

"You'll do," the woman says.

"That's it?" Gailya says before she can stop herself.

"This isn't chemistry. You'll make beds, clean tubs, and show up at seven every morning on the dot. Everything is high turnover in this part of town. If I waited for the best and brightest, I'd be up to my earrings in dirty linens. No offense." The woman laughs in a clipped way. "But I know you're not bothered. There's Derrica to show you how to do what's required." Gailya looks over to see a woman sweeping the hallway outside the administration suite. The woman nods to her.

Derrica is slim, taller than Gailya, with dark eyes that seem to look through Gailya's eyes to some point in the back of Gailya's skull. She is younger than Gailya. Too young.

Gailya spends the morning following Derrica around the bowels of the hotel. They join other women stocking the cleaning carts with essentials like face rags, shower caps, and little square chocolates for the deluxe suites. Gailya pockets a handful. Derrica is not talkative. It's afternoon, and they're on the thirteenth floor making a bed before Derrica says something not bed-making related.

"You need to put your back into everything." Derrica carries an armful of dirty sheets to the cart in the hall.

"Huh?"

Derrica continues when she returns. "I can tell wherever you come from this isn't your usual kind of work. But if you don't use your body right, you won't last long." She points at Gailya's shoulder. "This girl threw her shoulder out yesterday. That's why there was a job today."

"Thanks."

"I like your hair."

"Oh. Thank you." Gailya touches one of her own short braids, her neck flushing. And that's how their first day together goes.

When Gailya gets back home, a red poster is stuck on the window in her front door. The window is divided by frames, so the poster is rumpled by the frames, but she can read it. The city is notifying everyone that her house is on the bubble. Tax sale imminent. It's like pouring syrup on an ant pile. The buyers will go crazy crawling over themselves to get their feelers on her house. Gailya sticks her fingers in the gap behind the poster and pulls. Most of the poster is still there. She picks away a few more big pieces, but that just leaves the door window covered in bloody fragments.

The next morning, she returns to the casino hotel dressed in the gray-and-white maid's uniform that's too tight up top and too loose in the middle. She's not assigned to work with Derrica, but they're on the same floor together again. They start from opposite ends of the same hallway. Because Derrica is faster, her cart hopscotches from doorway to doorway until eventually it's pushed right next to Gailya's, almost touching. While Gailya wipes a mirror specked with bits of whatever the guests flossed from their teeth, she hears Derrica's vacuum through the wall. The vacuum sounds like a jumbo jet coming in for a landing. Gailya smiles at herself as her hands cross the mirror like the hands of a flagman.

Gailya moves to make the bed when she smells something funky. She pulls the sheets back from a bed and discovers a black furry thing. She screams.

"Yeah?" Derrica says, entering the room. Gailya is in the corner. She's standing halfway behind the drapes. She points to the bed. Derrica goes to the bed. She laughs. "You got Doolittle's room."

"Doolittle?"

"He stays here year-round." Derrica picks the thing up from the bed. "See, it's a gorilla mask."

Gailya exhales completely for the first time in minutes. "But why?"

"Don't know. He's some kind of poet or something, but he's okay. Always leaves a good tip. Most don't leave anything except more to clean up."

Gailya hadn't noticed a slip of paper on the nightstand. It's a thank-you note with ten dollars under it.

"What did you do to this mirror? It's all smudged." Derrica is in the bathroom, her voice echoing off the cream-colored tiles.

The bathroom still has some steam from when Gailya cleaned the tub and shower with hot water. But even with the mist, she can see the mirror is dirty looking. Derrica walks out and returns with a bottle.

"I'm not your boss, but if you want to keep people off your ass, use this. No streaks."

When Derrica gives Gailya the bottle of furniture polish, their hands graze, and the hairs on Gailya's arm stand up.

Over the next few days, Gailya does her picking-up-people-in-the-middle-of-the-night-job, mostly in a daze, as she waits for each new morning to go to the casino hotel. She tries not to be obvious with questions, but she learns that Derrica is not as young as she looks, only a few years younger than Gailya's forty-two. She grew up in the Lower Ninth Ward. Did short time in the Army, too, traveling to the Middle East, but hated being away from New Orleans. Is good with stringed instruments, most especially guitar. Derrica says she plays down on Frenchmen Street sometimes.

That Friday evening, Gailya drives her hatchback down Canal, makes an illegal left into the French Quarter. A clutch of state troopers watch her from their SUVs, but don't swarm. She works her way through oodles of night-time tourists buzzing between Jackson Square and the tourist trap beignet spot. She does love those beignets, though.

The app pings her to go pick up someone, a five-star rider looking for a ride way out to the airport—good money—but she ignores it. She turns off the app.

Inside the jazz club on Frenchmen, Gailya smells booze and the sad sweat of people trying to feel something real before they leave town. Drum and bass sounds vibrate from the stage like heat from pavement. Each note of the guitar sounds like honey drops off a dipper. Gailya can't see anything past a couple rows of swaying shoulders in polo shirts and pastel blouses. She stands on a rung at the bar and finds Derrica is onstage, wearing a snug blazer and fedora. That's her guitar sinning, Gailya thinks, noting the slip in her mind. She corrects herself. That's her guitar singing.

Derrica has control over the crowd like a snake charmer. When she speeds up, the room comes alive. When she slows down, they rock back and forth. It's during one of the dreamy sections, Gailya looks up to see Derrica staring right at her, even as Derrica's fingers continue to work the fret.

After the set, Gailya bides her time at the bar, sipping a beer. Waiting for what, she wonders. She's trying to get the bartender's attention to close out her tab when someone says her name. Gailya turns and sees that it's Derrica.

"So you came," Derrica says, biting her lip.

"I was around," Gailya says, trying to stay still on her seat.

"That's cool." Derrica makes a hand signal to the bartender. A moment later, a fresh cup of beer is in front of Gailya. Gailya says thank you. Derrica grabs her hand and gently turns Gailya toward her. Gailya's mind is swirling as if she were leaning over the side of a skyscraper. She's caught by the beauty of Derrica's face, the ridge of her lips, the tiny scar under her eye.

"I'm sitting in with the next band," Derrica says. "Maybe you can come by my place tomorrow night, I'm cooking."

"Like a date date?" Gailya asks.

"Like a date date," Derrica says.

Derrica's apartment is Uptown right next to the levee wall, across the street from a warehouse. It is one of only three houses on the block. Inside, Gailya and Derrica eat gumbo that Derrica spent the day making. It's good gumbo. The apartment is small. Could fit in the living room of Gailya's house. But it's clean smelling. They drink several glasses of wine, the flavor of which reminds her of sitting in a steaming bubble bath eating peaches.

"This whole thing with my house got me up at night," Gailya says. "Good-paying work is hard to find."

"So you don't think you'll ever go back to doing hair for a living?" Derrica asks.

"It just wasn't the same feeling after the storm. I don't know if the situation was all that different or if I was."

"I feel that. But you think you can help me with this?" Derrica points at her head.

Gailya hadn't said anything because she didn't want to be rude, but Derrica's edges are thin, and her long, box braids a puredee mess.

"I might be able to tighten you up." Gailya tips her almost-empty glass at Derrica.

Derrica raises an eyebrow. "Show me."

Gailya walks around the table and stands behind Derrica. She caresses several of her vanilla-scented braids, considering possibilities. She feels the warmth of Derrica's skin under her fingers.

"I'd need time for a redo. But right now, I could wrap it in a bun or put some down the side for that over-the-eye look." Gailya reaches forward to take a sip of Derrica's wine. But Derrica grabs Gailya's arm and pulls her into her body. Derrica wraps her arms around Gailya.

Gailya feels self-conscious about the fat of her belly and the way her thighs rub together, but the way Derrica strokes her tells Gailya that these are things Derrica likes about her body.

With warm breath on the back of her neck, Gailya relaxes into the curve of Derrica. It's been a while for Gailya. She and Coleen haven't hooked up in years, and the one or two stupid dates Gailya has been on since were a bust. But Gailya is ready when Derrica undoes the zipper on the back of the dress Gailya is wearing. Gailya unbuttons Derrica's button-down shirt and tosses it to the side. When they kiss, Gailya feels energized, and more than once that night, deep into the night, she will feel like she's grabbed one of the power lines the streetcars use.

"You sound, I don't know," Lea says over the phone the next night, "lighter, Mama."

"I just had a good few days, baby," Gailya says.

On a Tuesday, when Gailya is off, she goes to city hall to scream at, beg, or bribe whoever's holding the knife to her throat. She knows option three isn't a good option since she's still broke. But one of the old mayors went to prison for accepting a payoff of bricks, so anything is possible. She could give up the car to save her house.

She received a notice to come down for a hearing but is willing to bet it's all for show. So they can say they at least gave her a chance. Gailya sits in the back of the city council chamber. A man in a suit tells the people on the raised platform that his client's house is worth so many millions, but they can't expect him to pay all the many thousands they're asking for. One of the council members says they agree, a green light flashes on a desk. The lawyer turns around, does a little fist pump, and goes about his business.

Gailya is called. Actually, they don't say her name but say her home address, as if she is her house. After she hurries down the aisle and stops at the podium—she drops a bottle of allergy medicine from her purse and has to stop and pick it up—a councilwoman in pearls tells her to say her piece. Gailya feels tiny, the size of a mouse, tail pinched between the thumb and big finger of Councilwoman Pearls. Gailya plans to tell them about her house, mother, and grandmother, about her struggle to rebuild after the waters, about how people like *her* are what make New Orleans a place worth being.

"I've lived there my whole life—" she says, but Councilwoman Pearls holds up her hand.

"Wait one second, miss," a young male council member says, while a few of the other members whisper to each other behind hand-covered microphones.

"Our ruling would be—"

"Hold on, Ms. Council Lady," Gailya says.

"Oh, we're not the council," Councilwoman Pearls says.

Gailya glances around at the seven people staring at her. "Who are you people?"

"We're the housing taxation and blight subcommittee."

"My house ain't blighted. I just had it painted a couple years ago."

Councilwoman Pearls jots something on a pad Gailya can't see. "Miss, we're going to continue this hearing so that you can get some assistance."

"So they let you off the hook?" Derrica says. They're shaking their booties in a second line parade under the Claiborne Avenue overpass, just a few blocks from Gailya's house. The brass band is a block away and hundreds of people fill the space between the two of them and the band. A bunch of women dressed like baby dolls are going wild in the middle of the street.

"Just till I get a lawyer or somebody. I looked like a puredee fool." Gailya puts a hand on her hip and shakes it. She hates second lines. Well, *hate* is too strong a way to say it. But she dislikes all the noise and chaos. The people bumping into your face with their elbows, stepping on your feet. But the brass band is strong, and Gailya is feeling it today.

It was Derrica who convinced her to come. Gailya feels like she's getting some kind of proof about what kind of girl Derrica is. Derrica who has a daiquiri in one hand and a gold handkerchief in the other. A real New Orleans woman. Can't nobody fake that.

Gailya is no slouch. She has a frilly, white umbrella. She can dance, really dance. It's in the bones of her hips and feet, her mother used to say, handed down to her by all their ancestors. Derrica dances herself, her whole body going from soft to ridged and back again. Her feet jittering almost too fast to see. She looks like a spider on the hunt. Her head bobbing, her shoulders flexing, makes Gailya feel like a fly in a web, silk around her throat, welcoming the sting of those fangs.

"That's what you are," Derrica says, "*my* fool."

The day after the second line, Gailya and Derrica arrive in Gailya's car at the casino hotel employee garage. The gate won't rise. They park a couple of blocks away by a meter Gailya can't afford to pay, but the city won't tow it, even if the ticket wipes out a chunk of a day's pay.

At the side door of the hotel, they come up on a group of their co-workers, some other maids, kitchen staff and fixers, too.

"What's up with this?" Derrica says.

Big Lev, the morning crew grill man who always saves them a cut of breakfast steak or diced sausages, shrugs. "Don't know, but I ain't liking this. Door locked on payday ain't no kind of good."

The white lady in the rose-colored glasses pulls up in a compact on the same level as Gailya's car. Gailya assumed she was rich, that she drives a slick luxury ride, but not so. She climbs out of the dusty-gray car; her stringy brown hair is messy, all over her head. She pulls down the hem of her skirt and tries to make her hair look normal. Walking to the door, she says nothing to the workers, but faintly nods. She types a code into the pad by the door, and nothing happens. She takes off her glasses and rubs her face. The woman's eyes are small and beady.

"It's true then," she says. "The company is in receivership. We've been shut down."

"Receiver-what?" Derrica says.

"They ain't pay they bills," Gailya says.

"Does that mean we don't get paid?" Derrica says. "Hello? Boss lady?" Derrica swears. Gailya touches Derrica's arm.

The next afternoon, Gailya sits in a fine room in a big house on State Street. A yellow-haired lady with pedicured toenails sits across from her on a long velvet bench. Gailya is there to answer a call for an au pair. But she's no fool. She knows that title doesn't apply to her. Au pairs are little foreign white girls with names like Anne and Sophie. Women like her who have done this work for centuries are mammies.

"So you'd need me to cook and clean and stuff?" Gailya says. She's distracted by the lady's blue-green toenails. The exact same color as the baby bath she used to wash Lea in.

"No, not at all." The yellow-haired lady flicks her fingers as she talks. Like she's tugging strings connected to rooms all over the house and all over the city. "Sara comes each morning and handles the general cleaning. You know, the main bedrooms upstairs and the den and Paul's study, although he typically uses his downtown office by Lafayette

Square anyway. We use a service for most of the meals unless I choose to make dinner. You would just get the kids ready for school, walk them over and back afterward, tidy their rooms, prepare healthy snacks—I have a binder of approved snacks—take them to the park. That sort of thing."

"Well, I can handle that." Gailya adjusts her body on the soft sofa. There's too much give; it'll swallow her if she relaxes.

"Good," the lady says. "When that poor Sudanese girl's visa was denied, I was floored. What's happening to the world, I just don't know!" The lady grabs her own knee and shakes her head. "It's a real shame. But never mind all that. I'm so glad Reverend Smith recommended you. You know, ever since he's been on the board of the art foundation, he's been such a darling. I just love him. And I just know you'll love Molly and Charlie. They're little darlings, you know."

Gailya is given a tour of the house—it's large and beautiful, but nothing she hadn't seen in her years of catering work. She is relieved to learn that there's no uniform strictly speaking, but there is a dress code. She's to wear the kinds of clothes caretakers in hospitals, nursing homes, and nurseries wear. Loose, plain tops. Dark pants or long skirts. Nothing flashy, clingy, or flesh presenting. Her new boss, Aimee, wants her to start that same day. What Gailya is wearing, a scoop-neck blouse, is seemingly too flashy for Aimee's guidelines. Aimee tells Gailya to help herself to whatever she likes from a box of clothes that she's been meaning to donate to the shelter by the expressway.

Gailya would never have put on the clothes without washing them first, but Aimee hands Gailya an advance check for the first week, which is how she winds up at a private elementary school a quarter mile away wearing another woman's clothes.

Aimee insists Gailya leave her own car and take the Land Rover, as it has something like twenty airbags and enough road clearance to bring her children home if a flash flood occurs, which occasionally happens. Gailya parks the SUV in front of the school. A bell chimes and chirren bounce down the steps. Gailya realizes she's doesn't even know what small, pale faces to look for. She'd only glimpsed at the family photos on the mantel and end tables. Gailya is texting Aimee to ask her to send some pictures of her offspring when the back door of the SUV pops open. A little girl climbs into the back of the vehicle. An older, not by much, girl climbs into the front seat.

"Let's roll," the older girl, yellow haired like her mother, says.

Gailya stares at the girl for a moment. These white chirren, Gailya thinks, and shifts the Land Rover to drive. If Lea had gotten into a car with a stranger, Gailya would have told her all kinds of things about protecting herself from strangers. But the girl just sits back in the seat, her feet dangling, like it's an everyday occurrence. This whole situation with Aimee is like that nightmare Gailya used to have in high school: She's taking a test but her pencil keeps melting in her hand. When she asks for a new pencil, the teacher screeches like a bat.

* * *

It had been almost five days since she last saw Derrica. In texts, Derrica said she was busy searching for work herself and spending time jamming with other musicians. But the clipped way their texts went had Gailya thinking their time apart wasn't just a coincidence. She was on the wrong side of other people's boredom enough times to know what it might mean. Gailya is trying not to sweat it, and failing.

"I can't believe you've been dating this chick for weeks and didn't even tell me," Coleen says. They're at the fast-food chicken spot on Canal Street between the souvenir shop and Seth Jansen's, a restaurant where the customers and waiters dress the same way: in sleek blacks and grays. It was a hassle to find parking, but Gailya had a roll of quarters to feed the meter, and needed someone to talk to and some salty, greasy, crunchy food to calm her mind.

"Everything ain't about you," Gailya says, dunking fried chicken crust into the red beans and rice. The headache in her temples is back again for the fourth day straight.

"I get it." Coleen scoops coleslaw into her mouth. "She sounds like a good time and nice and everything. I just figured you'd tell me. She could have been a serial killer and murdered you and you could have been dead on your kitchen floor and I wouldn't have known anything until you showed up on the internet."

"That's fine anyway," Gailya says. "She got other things on her mind lately."

Coleen grabs Gailya's hand. Coleen's hand is sticky from

barbeque sauce. "This girl really has gotten her barb in you." Gailya starts to pull her hand back, but lets Coleen have it.

"I'm stuck. What can I do? I ain't trying to be all up in the face of someone who ain't interested."

"Maybe you're wrong. She could be depressed about you two getting shitcanned by that hotel. She might be lying around in her panties drinking rye all day. Let her tell you what the deal is. Can't know if you don't ask."

Gailya drives down Tchoupitoulas in the direction of Derrica's apartment. She tells herself that she's just an old, broke, short, soon-to-be-homeless, college-dropout mammie. She thinks she is not, and cannot be, enough for Derrica. She almost turns away from Derrica's dead-end street, but notices Derrica's lights are on. Her first-floor apartment faces the street. Gailya sees movement. Gailya parks two houses down, and looks around to see if anyone is walking around the block. Not seeing anyone, she creeps onto Derrica's porch, stepping as lightly as she can. Through a gap in the blinds covering the front window she sees the interior of the front room, smoky from weed Gailya can smell through the glass. Derrica is at the head of her table. A woman—short, thick, and dark like Gailya, but much younger and with long black extensions—steps into view. Not even good extensions, but ones that look like old-ass seaweed. The woman caresses Derrica's shoulders. Just as they are about to kiss, the porch squeaks under Gailya's shifting feet. She runs back to her hatchback.

The next couple of weeks spin past like this: Most mornings she's at the McAdam household by six. She puts on a pot of oatmeal or makes an egg-white omelet with wheat toast if it's a weekend. She wakes up Aimee and Paul's chirren. She makes sure they brush their teeth and wash their faces. She gets them dressed. She helps them pack their school bags. She feeds them oatmeal with slices of fruit on the side and OJ or almond milk to wash it down. She makes sure they kiss their parents bye, brings them to school, and drops them off. She goes back to the McAdam house and eats whatever is leftover from breakfast. Spends the morning cleaning up Molly's and Charlie's bedrooms. She puts the toys in their cubbyholes. Straightens the girls' desks and nightstands. She makes their beds, unless one of them wet the bed, which happens to one of them at least once a week. She runs a load of clothes or bedsheets. She eats a leftover shrimp po'boy or a leftover hot sausage sandwich, from the night before, for lunch with a bag of spicy chips and a cold drink. She throws the load of the chirren's clothes in the dryer. Washes another load. Picks up any other toys or belongings of the girls that are in the common areas. She dries the second load. Folds the clothes. Sometimes Sara with the cleaning service is around to mop the kitchen and bathrooms, vacuum the carpeted areas. She's nice enough. But her English is less than and Gailya doesn't know any Spanish at all except to say *hola*, nice to see you. Gailya wonders who cares about Sara, whether she has a family here, or maybe she's here a million miles from home. Sometimes Aimee is around but usually she's off doing

Pilates, jogging up St. Charles with the streetcars, or lunching and drinking with her girlfriends at Commander's Palace. She sells makeup products, but Gailya never sees her selling. Gailya picks up the chirren from school. Feeds them a snack of chopped fruits or a quinoa mix or a half serving of chia pudding. She helps them do their homework. She clocks their free-play time. Sixty minutes each night. Ninety minutes if there's a playdate with one of the chirren from nearby. Gailya logs Molly and Charlie's dinner even when they eat with their own parents or at other families' houses. They're old enough to bathe themselves, but she ensures they have towels, soap, and powders. She gets them to their beds, so their parents can say good night, if they want. Gailya says good night to the McAdams. By the third week this even includes accepting a kiss from the younger one, Molly. Gailya drives across town toward her house, picks up two or three riders on the app along the way to keep the money rolling. She always passes by Derrica's, even though it's a waste of gas. She always stops at the corner of Derrica's house and stares until another car comes along and honks. Sometimes Derrica's lights are on. Sometimes they're off. Gailya then drives to pick up a po'boy, fries, a daiquiri, and dessert from the po'boy shop by her house. She checks the rental side of her house to see if whatever renters were there left the place in one piece. She cleans that side of her house and leaves a key in the flowerpot for the next visitors. She eats half a po'boy, all the fries, and drinks the daiquiri. She also eats a bowl of banana pudding or bread pudding, depending on what the shop had. She usually falls asleep with the pudding and spoon on her stomach and sometimes dreams of people wrapping her house in caution tape.

But the money is good. She's stacking more than she did in catering. If she can hang on long enough, she might be able to pay off a big enough hunk of her taxes. It's a better look than the unpleasant alternatives she's fantasized about, like showing up in Japan and asking Lea to take her in. Gailya would rather die. It's not that Lea would turn her away. It's that Lea is just getting started. And Gailya knows almost nothing of Lea's real problems, the things Lea won't say to keep Gailya from worrying. Gailya won't be another burden on that invisible list.

One morning, as Gailya is leaving home for the McAdams', she stands on the sidewalk and stretches out her back, which has been tight lately. A white man on the steps of John Jackets's old house waves and says "Howdy." Her rude neighbor on the next block is playing his morning trumpet music as usual. This time he's playing Chocolate Milk. Gailya curses them both under her breath, but waves back at the white man as she drives off.

Gailya kneels on the hardwood in the foyer of the McAdam house. She's trying to slip rain boots over Molly's shoes since it's pouring outside.

"I need you to point your toes, baby," Gailya says, huffing.

"She's just making it difficult so you'll take more time with her," Charlie says from the doorway.

"Charlene McAdam, do you have your book bag?" Gailya says. Lightning crashes outside.

"I always have my bag," Charlie says. "Do you have your bag?" Gailya screws up her mouth to say something, but Molly pats her cheek.

"How are you going to keep us from getting wet?" Molly says.

"You going to get wet, baby. But you won't drown."

After Gailya drops the girls off, she drives to her lawyer's office. The lawyer is light-skinned with high cheeks, like a laughing cat statue. His office is in back of a house near City Park, on the other side of town from the McAdams'. He keeps opening and closing the manila folder with the papers she got from the hearing at city hall.

"You should have brought this to me sooner," he says. "They got you set for reappearance in two days." Gailya knows she should have come earlier. But every time she went to call him her body froze up. Or she found something else to do with her time, like checking her mattress for spiders.

"I know that," Gailya say, "but can you help?"

"Don't worry. We'll work this out. But I'm gonna need that retainer to start."

Gailya counts off a bunch of those silly-looking Monopoly-money hundred-dollar bills. That's a nasty wad of what she spent the last forever saving. But what is all the saving for, if not the house?

As she leaves the lawyer's office, her phone chimes. It's Coleen. They haven't spoken in weeks. Coleen showed up at Gailya's house the other day, but Gailya locked herself in the bathroom for an hour to avoid her. She ignores the call.

She doesn't want to feel the embarrassment of explaining that she doesn't know how to explain anything.

That night, after she leaves the McAdams', Gailya goes to a bar in Gentilly with a pole in the middle of the floor. The pole is not for dancers. It holds up the roof. There's a good crowd out, but not as packed as when she went down to Frenchmen Street last month. She saw a flyer on the wall when she was buying a po'boy. Derrica Smalls and the Flow.

When Derrica's set is over, Gailya watches her take compliments from the audience. A woman hands her a beer. That's when Gailya locks eyes with Derrica. Gailya doesn't want to be that person, but here she is, and she doesn't know who else to be. Derrica tells the woman something that seems to make the woman who gave her the beer turn around and walk back to her stool.

"'Sup," Derrica says.

"'Sup?" Gailya says. Gailya sees the other woman staring at her from across the room. "Let's talk for a minute, Derrica Smalls." They go outside where cars and motorcycles are double-parked. A bunch of women are hanging out and joking. A big iron grill cooks hamburger patties and ribs.

"Well?" Derrica looks around without focusing on Gailya.

"You stopped answering," Gailya says, noting Derrica's mouth, her brisk smell, the way her own body feels a few degrees warmer in her presence. "I didn't know you was this kind of player. I guess that's why I came. To be sure."

"Hey, it's not like that. I've had it crazy and with this tour coming up, no time at all."

"Tour?"

"I leave for New York in a few days." Derrica places a hand on Gailya's hip. "You should stop by my place tomorrow night." Suddenly, Derrica's scent is filling Gailya's brain. Gailya imagines a hot-air balloon rising toward the sky. She shakes her head.

"I don't think you hearing me." Gailya pushes Derrica's hand away and steps free. "I came to tell you goodbye."

"Whoa whoa whoa. Calm down, shorty. It don't have to be that way."

"Fuck you, Derrica," Gailya says. She flips Derrica the bird as she walks down the block to her car.

Gailya speeds off too fast. She blows through a light, the needle on the dashboard past the red line. She thinks she can go faster until the car explodes like a hard-boiled egg in a microwave. Lea's calling. Gailya wants to let it go to voicemail, but never misses her daughter's calls, if she has a choice. She breaks hard and pulls to the side of the road, huffing. She pounds the dash once and answers.

"Konichiwa, Mama," Lea says brightly.

"Konichiwa, baby." Gailya laughs. It makes her happy to say hello to her child in somebody else's way. "You calling late. Everything alright?"

"School's out so I'm at the pachinko parlor with my co-workers."

"Let me ask you something serious, Lea Maribel."

Gailya only uses Lea's middle name when she wants her complete attention. "How happy are you right now?"

"Right this second, Mama? I'm not sure. Are you okay?"

"I just had a long day, baby. One to ten it for me."

"I'm doing what I enjoy. I have good friends. I can recite Jamaica Kincaid in Japanese now. Oh. And I just sent you a pic before I called!" Gailya puts the phone on speaker and opens the picture. Lea is with a group of smiling people. She's wearing shiny armor and has big metal wings. "I'll give it a ten, Mama. That's how I feel right now. Mama, was that a hiccup? Mama, are you crying?"

"No, baby, I'm just fine." Inching her car into drive, she wipes her cheek.

Back on her own porch, Gailya sits drinking a daiquiri. Two more of those "I want to buy your house" letters were waiting for her when she got home. The latest ones promise to pay well over market price to cover any debts the owner might have, and then some.

It's almost midnight. She's off tomorrow and bought a party jug daiquiri, and the jug is almost empty. She doesn't want to think about the hangover she'll have in the morning or the sugar diabetes she might catch if she doesn't cut back. She glances at the houses to her left and right, unsettled by the quiet. She used to do this, sit on her porch in the middle of the night, all the time when she was younger. It felt safer before. She realizes her former neighbors were a big part of why she felt so comfortable doing this back then.

"Ms. Gailya," a young man in baggy jeans and a tank top says, walking up the block. Gailya grabs the arm of her chair. She doesn't know him. He's not from the neighborhood. The boy pulls an envelope from his slouchy jeans. "Mr. Ivey asked me to give this to you."

"Who?"

"Your lawyer up on Carrollton."

"Oh. Why didn't he mail it?"

"I'm faster than the mail," the young man says. "He put in the box, you get it in two days. He give it to me, you got it now."

Gailya opens the letter under her porch light. The letter says the city has reassessed her house. She owes even more than they thought before. Gailya inhales and crumples the letter, feeling the sharp paper edges against her skin. It's like the city is pranking her, putting plastic wrap over the toilet and stuffing her nightstand with rubber snakes. Gailya pulls the cap off her daiquiri jug and wonders if it isn't time to just give in. All the money she's spending might be better spent on a small apartment in the suburbs near the mall. She downs the rest of the daiquiri.

That Thursday afternoon Gailya is in the passenger seat of Aimee McAdam's SUV, for a trip to Magazine Street for snowballs. Aimee drives and the chirren are in back. Charlie has on her headphones and is watching a video on her phone. Molly plays with a pair of plush toys, a cat and a bug.

The impact of the other car is enough to spin the SUV backward. Gailya's vision is blurry for a moment, then corrects. She unhooks her seatbelt and looks back. The girls are still in their places. They'd dropped their distractions, and Charlie's mouth is wide open like she's unsure whether to laugh or cry.

"It's okay, babies," Gailya says.

Aimee rubs her forehead and grunts. She looks at Gailya with frantic eyes. "Shit shit shit! You've got to swap with me."

"What?"

"This is my third accident in five years. They'll put me away. I'm under the influence."

"The influence of what?"

Aimee glances back at her daughters. She spells out the word *marijuana* fast like a rapper trying to stay ahead of the beat. "Gailya, look. That man in the other car is still out of sorts. Any second he's going to see me in this driver's seat and then I'm screwed. I'll pay you whatever you ask. You want enough for a new car? Done. Bail money for one of your people in jail. I'll pay it."

Gailya knows Aimee is serious. Even with her racist comment, Gailya considers her offer. The money she needs to pay off her increased taxes is just a weekend trip for them. But she isn't about to go to anyone's jail. House or no house.

"Ain't none of my family in jail."

"What?" Aimee says.

"You heard me," Gailya says. "I ain't doing it."

"You black bitch!"

Aimee breathes out hard and looks back at her daughters with a *Can you believe this?* face. She turns the key, but the Land Rover won't start. She yells and presses her head against the steering wheel. Gailya takes the girls out of the vehicle and waits with them on the sidewalk for the police to come.

Aimee is taken away, so Gailya waits at the house with the girls until Paul shows up. He asks her to stay, but she does only until a friend of their family arrives. She puts on the maid uniform she still has from the hotel that is in her car trunk. Then she leaves her work outfits in the washroom, tells the girls bye—Charlie acts like she doesn't care, but Molly cuts up crying—and writes a note telling the McAdams she hopes they have a nice life.

At 11 P.M., Gailya goes to pick up her bus. Someone she knows has a party bus and asked her to run groups around the city. She's been doing this on weekends. At 2:20 A.M., Gailya picks up about fifteen people at a karaoke bar in the French Quarter. A couple are Black, but the group is mostly white. She flips on the strobe lights, cranks up the bounce music, and drives the long, wide vehicle around downtown, the cabin rocking like a ship. Some of the white girls try to twerk. As they pass the Superdome for the second time, a white boy with bright teeth leans next to her, his hand on the back of the driver's seat, and yells over the music.

"Hey, no offense," he says. "Can I ask why you're dressed that way?"

Gailya glances down at herself. She hadn't even realized

that she was still wearing the maid uniform. Gailya laughs. "I'm a maid."

The white boy throws his arms up like he won something. "I love this town," he yells. "Wooo!"

After a couple hours of sleep, Gailya gets up at 6 A.M. She opens her ride-sharing app and drives a few people back to their hotels from the French Quarter. Around 9 A.M., she goes to the office of that lawyer whose name she can't remember. She walks up the steps to the back of the house where the office entrance is located, but the door is locked. She peers through the glass and the house is empty. She places her hands on her knees and breathes in but doesn't exhale.

That evening, Gailya wakes up to the sound of a knock on the door. She folds her housecoat over her body and pats her hair. When she opens the door, a half dozen white people are on her porch. She doesn't say a word, but stares for a moment. It's the most white people she's seen in one place at one time on her block since the summer after the storm. Back then, passenger vans were spitting clumps of white teenagers all over the city—church volunteers from the Midwest and Lord knows where else, come to gut houses and help rebuild. It strikes her that these people could be some of the same kids just grown up.

"Are y'all Methodists?" Gailya says. The group looks at each other. A tall brown-haired man talks first.

"No," he says. "I'm Tucker. I live over there in the peach-colored one." He points across the street, the house that had been John Jackets's house.

"And we're the Smarts," the chubby, dark-haired girl says. "Patty and John. We moved in next door last month." Mr. Dexter's house. "And that's Willem and Ellen."

"We have the one on the corner," the woman in pink tights says. Retired Principal Holmes's family house.

"Is there a problem?" Gailya says.

"No problem at all," the tall brown-haired man says. "But we noticed you hadn't responded to our flyers." Gailya saw some flyers over the past few weeks and tossed them in the trash.

"And who are y'all again?" Gailya says.

"We're the neighborhood association," the tall brown-haired man says.

"Since when?" There was already an association, although Gailya realized that most of the active members were no longer around. "Are y'all the ones trying to buy this house?"

"No," the girl with the cheeks says. "We thought it's good to be engaged together."

"So we just wanted to invite you to our meeting. It starts in fifteen minutes at the coffee shop." Gailya didn't know any of these people. They'd just told her their names, and she'd already forgot them. But if they are trying to do things, she needs to know.

"What coffee shop?" Gailya says.

The chubby woman points away from Gailya. "On Villere around the corner there." The woman says *Vil-leer* like some kind of robot instead of the proper *Vil-er-ry*. The coffee shop had been the po'boy shop. She went there one day weeks ago, and it was closed. The po'boy shop sold phone cards, lottery tickets, and po'boys. They took 'lectric light bill payments and wired money places. Things people needed. Now, there's a drawing of a po'boy, like a science man might make, with details of where to insert the fried shrimps, where to put the mayonnaise.

Gailya shows up thirty minutes later, after she gets dressed, and buys something called pierogi. She finds a two-top table with silver chairs off to the side. While she eats it, she plays like she's on her phone to avoid the ones trying to chat. Gailya's new neighbors talk among themselves for a few minutes. Their little meeting is at a big wooden table, at the center of the shop. She sits off to the side and eats. She likes the pierogi. They remind her of the dumplings they sell at the Vietnamese place near the bridge.

The tall man with the brown hair is talking. "Karen and I will be doing a trash pick-up this weekend starting at eight A.M. As you know, we've got a wee bit of a problem with people discarding packaging on the ground. But we think that if we consistently engage, it may encourage others to be more mindful of our shared environment."

Gailya absentmindedly notices that she's nodding. Trifling folks have been junking up the blocks for so long. It's about time someone is doing something about it.

"There are other matters, but I think we should skip to the one that's been on all our minds. Ellen, you have some information."

The one in the pink tights stands. "Thanks, Tucker. I called and spoke to the quality-of-life officer at the police district. He said that if they get enough calls then maybe they can do something."

"That's great news," the chubby-cheeked girl says. Gailya looks back and forth and Pink Tights notices.

"Oh, dearie," Pink Tights says. "Sorry. Noise pollution. There's a man who plays his trumpet from the steps of his house. He's one street over from you and me. But Samantha says she can hear it several streets away."

Gailya looks at the faces of her new neighbors, most of whom look like people she's worked for at one point or another. She knows that if any of her old neighbors were here, they would make them understand. But she realizes it falls on her. It always fell on her, and that if she were gone, nobody would ever come to understand anything at all.

"Did y'all try talking to him?"

"Pardon?" the brown-haired man says.

"He's a music teacher, and his playing ain't no trouble." Gailya stands. "Those chirren from those schools down the block used to live all over the neighborhood. You couldn't walk without seeing somebody chirren practicing on they trombone or snare drum. I miss those noisy chirren. Now, that was noise. I bet you could've heard them all the way by Lake Pontchartrain." Gailya is shaking her head and smiling to herself, but realizing she's not making her point.

"What was your name?" she asks the brown-haired one.

"Tucker," he says.

"Where you come from?"

"Portland, Oregon."

"I don't know that place, but you moved here. You know we got Mardi Gras and Jazz Fest and all those things. How you think all those musicians learn how to play? It's cause they always playing. Day and night. Hurricane or shine. This is New Orleans." A young woman wiping a table across the room smiles at Gailya.

"We'll take that under consideration," Tucker says.

The next morning, Gailya is brushing her teeth when the music stops. She walks out of her back door, toothpaste foam on her mouth. From her back porch, she sees her rude neighbor who plays the music talking to three policemen, trumpet dangling from his hand. She realizes she hasn't seen him in years—he's gone bald—but he's still the same gangly brother in camo shorts. She closes the door and rinses her mouth in the bathroom sink.

Gailya hears something at the front door. There are shadows on the frosted windowpane that suggest moving bodies and, from the distance coming closer, a jazz beat from bass and snares. When Lea heard that music, she would run to the window and watch the brass band pass. But Gailya wants more. Gailya will be in the crush of bodies when it turns the corner to the next block, thousands of arms, legs, and eyes reaching for a bell of brass.

Acknowledgments

Writing these stories was a journey that spanned more than a decade of my life. I thank everyone who helped make this book possible. Special thank-you to my agent, PJ Mark; my editor at One World, Nicole Counts; and Victory Matsui, who acquired this work, and to the cover designer, Michael Morris. Thank you also to my writing group, the Peauxdunque Writers Alliance, and the editorial board at the *Peauxdunque Review*. And to my family—Tanzanika, Ma, and all y'all—thank you for your constant support.

Further thanks to the institutions and organizations that supported this work: the University of New Orleans Creative Writing Workshop, the University of Mississippi John and Renée Grisham Writers in Residence program, Louisiana State University Department of English, Voices of Our Nations Arts Foundation, Randolph College MFA, the Center for Fine Arts (Brussels), Tulane University Department of English, Susquehanna University Department of English and Creative Writing, Maine Media, *The Iowa Review*, Duotrope, and the Pirate's Alley Faulkner Society.

About the Author

MAURICE CARLOS RUFFIN is the author of *We Cast a Shadow*, which was a finalist for the PEN/Faulkner Award, the PEN/Open Book Award, and the Dayton Literary Peace Prize and long-listed for the Center for Fiction First Novel Prize and International Dublin Literary Award. A recipient of an Iowa Review Award in fiction, he has been published in the *Virginia Quarterly Review*, *AGNI*, the *Kenyon Review*, *The Massachusetts Review*, and *Unfathomable City: A New Orleans Atlas*. A native of New Orleans, he is a graduate of the University of New Orleans Creative Writing Workshop and a member of the Peauxdunque Writers Alliance.

Twitter: @MauriceRuffin
Instagram: @mauriceruffin
facebook.com/mauricecarlosruffin

About the Type

This book was set in Baskerville, a typeface designed by John Baskerville (1706–75), an amateur printer and typefounder, and cut for him by John Handy in 1750. The type became popular again when the Lanston Monotype Corporation of London revived the classic roman face in 1923. The Mergenthaler Linotype Company in England and the United States cut a version of Baskerville in 1931, making it one of the most widely used typefaces today.